Two Broken Hearts...

DOMINIQUE THOMAS

Am I Good Enough to Love?

Author's Note

Disclaimer: This is a re-release of a previously titled book No More Broken Hearts that was also written by me. If you read that book before then enjoy it again and if you haven't and this is your first time reading that book, then welcome to Jordyn and Vadah's world!

I wrote this book a year ago, ladies on my phone. I had just completed a collab with BriAnn Danae, another talented author, and Jordyn spoke to me. The collab was Jordyn's mother and aunts' book. Jordyn's voice was so strong I wrote her book on my Word app, and here we are now. I want you all to read this story because it's just that good. It's sad, it's funny, and it's brutally honest. Every parent won't love you the way you need them to. Life won't always be good, and your heart won't always be whole.

Sometimes it will be broken. Then it's up to you on how you wanna repair it. You can let the pieces stay apart or slowly put them back together. Jordyn and Zion are everything to me, and now I introduce you to them. All I ask is that you leave a Review and download the book Am I Good

Enough to Love, which is her mother and aunts' book that I co-wrote with the beautiful and talented BriAnn Danae. If you haven't read any of her work, then do so, ladies. You're missing out! Here's the link to the book that's connected with this one. Am I Good Enough To Love

she was powerful,
not because she wasn't scared
but because she went on so strongly,
despite the fear
-Atticus-

CHAPTER

One

THE SLOW LEAK from the ceiling was like a dreary soundtrack to death. Ragged breathing and murderous thoughts were Zion's makeup at the moment. His russet hued eyes ascended to the shitty ass ceiling before peering back down at the man before him.

Inhumane thoughts plagued Zion's mental as his steel toed boots paced the blood splattered pavement. It was scary what one would do if pushed to their limit. It was easy to stay jovial and upstanding while living in a perfect world, but he wasn't. Zion's life was far from that, and the world he once had happiness in was no more.

He closed his eyes and sighed.

Could he do this?

Would he?

Zion's thoughts flash backed to *her*, and their last conversation. His heart raced at an unnatural rate.

Clutter filled the home as a loud Sativa strain floated through the stuffy air. Zion glanced around in disgust before shaking his head.

"When was the last time you cleaned this muthafucka?"

Dayana's almond shaped eyes peered up at Zion, and she

shrugged. She gave him a small smile, and he admired her natural beauty. One big enough to expose her dimples but not wide enough to show off her pretty white teeth.

No, they couldn't be together, but that didn't mean he no longer cared for her. It was clear that a relationship between them wouldn't survive, but their friendship had. They'd been friends since the seventh grade, and she was like one of his boys. Also, she'd given him something irreplaceable.

"Please, I've been working, and I'm beyond tired. I'm also having boyfriend issues," her light voice replied.

Zion stopped inspecting the apartment to look down at her. "What I say the first time I met that nigga?"

Dayana rolled her eyes, and Zion nodded. He overlooked her pretty face, racy attire, and stared into her eyes.

Even as a teen, she never quite knew her worth.

That didn't sit right with him.

"He's not good enough for you, Yana," he replied.

"And just how would you know that?"

Zion sat on the cluttered La-Z-Boy and placed his russet shaded eyes on Dayana. His intense stare made her swallow hard.

"Because no man who loves you is gonna make you cry continually. I keep telling you, Yana, that it's not what a nigga is telling you, it's what he does that shows he cares. Every time I hit you up, you're in pain. Yeah, couples go through it, but it's not normal to always be beefing with your spouse. I'm not an expert on love, but even I know that shit ain't cool. He done fucked around on you and everything. You and I both know what you need to do with this, man," he replied while looking her way.

Dayana's leg began to bounce as she frowned at Zion. Her lips grew into a thin line, and she rolled her eyes. She loved Zion's honesty. She often praised him for being able to speak the truth no matter what. However, when his blunt attitude was aimed her way, she loathed it.

Dayana scoffed before shaking her head.

"You're not perfect. Don't let these clueless ass broads who chase

you convince you otherwise. What he and I have is real. He's good to me, and maybe if you had someone special in your life, you would understand that, but you don't. You don't have anyone to go home to, but that's not my fault…" Dayana stopped talking and abruptly stood up.

"You know what? You need to leave. I can't deal with your disrespectful ass any longer. Please go, Zion," she angrily said.

Zion slowly stood and brushed a hand over his fade. He peered down at Dayana and nodded.

"It's all good. You know it's all love, ma. I was here before him, and I'll be here for you after him. Relax," he replied before leaving her place.

Zion shook his head to rid his thought of her.

A mildew scent clung to the thick air as he glanced down at the man.

"You ready to talk?"

The man snorted. Fear danced in his dark eyes, but he was putting on a front. Trying to be brave in his last moments, and Zion couldn't do shit but respect that.

"I told you what I know. Do it. If that's what you feel you need to do, then pull the fucking trigger!"

Spittle flew from the angry man's mouth as he replied. Zion lit his blunt as he stared down at him intently.

He was angry.

Frustrated as fuck that once again his leads had led him to a dead end. It was like he was chasing a ghost, and, in a sense, he was. Because the minute he found the person responsible for his pain, he would end their life.

He'd done a lot in his twenty-one years of living but killing hadn't been one of them. Still, he was ready to take that leap.

For them, he had to.

"Oh, nigga, death is coming for your ass. Don't worry 'bout that. I'm more concerned about this Al cat you were talking 'bout. Where the fuck he at?"

The tied-up man shrugged. His expensive outfit clung to his sweaty frame while urine soiled his jeans. His feet ached like a muthafucka in his $2000 shoes, and all he could think about was why he'd wasted his life on so much bullshit? He'd spent his spare time with his hoes, his boys, and blew through money like it was water.

Now, as death came around the corner looking for him, he couldn't recall the last time he'd verbally told his wife he loved her. He felt like shit. His head fell as he accepted his fate. He was certain hell was waiting for him.

Shit, he'd done nothing good to make it to heaven.

"Al works for Ty'Shawn. His street name is Tye, and he runs shit in Southwest. He put the hit out on your girls, and you know how the rest go."

Ty'Shawn aka Tye.

Got it.

Zion thought with a curt nod. He tossed out his blunt before trudging over to his victim. This was the first real lead he had, and he was grateful for it.

"Thanks for the info," Zion said and pushed the needle into the man's arm.

He injected him with a drug that immediately stopped the man's racing heart.

Zion closed his eyes and said a small prayer.

"Search me, God, and you know my heart. Try me, and you know my thoughts," he murmured.

This wasn't him; this was never the life he'd intended to have, but life happened, and now the only thing he could do was roll with the punches.

One body.

One soul, he'd taken, and what scared Zion was that he felt no remorse. Already, his soul was turning black.

"How is the one on Eight Mile and Mound doing?"

Jewel looked at Zion and smiled. She was a shitty employee, but she was pretty to look at and knew mad niggas who stopped by the dispensary, so Zion let her keep her job. He watched her closely, though, because the second she wasn't an asset to him, her ass was kicking rocks.

"All the dispensaries are doing great. Do you need *anything*?" Her question came out sultry and was laced with lust.

Jewel parted her lips and gave Zion a sexy smirk as she stood to her feet.

Zion looked up from his papers, and his eyes fell on her. Working and hunting was getting the best of him. Weariness showed all over his handsome, mocha shaded face. He shook his head, not bothering to pick up the shit she was tossing his way.

"Nah, I'm good. You can shut down shop for the day," he replied.

Jewel nodded, trying to keep a smile on her pretty face. She'd once again been burned by Zion as he brushed off her advances. She exited his office, and before she could shut the door, his brother was walking in. Zeke stood tall, much bigger than his older brother, Zion, and that was saying a lot, considering that Zion was 6'3". By his side was a strikingly beautiful young woman with eyes so enchanting that Zion had to sit back in his seat and openly admire her beauty.

"What up, boy! I see you once again in this muthafucka

slaving. You the only nigga I know that works on a Saturday and shit. Like you don't own the company," Zeke said, slapping hands with Zion.

Zion chuckled. No matter what, his brother had a way of making him laugh. Zeke was known as the jokester of the family, and with so much darkness in his life, Zion appreciated his presence.

"Shit, you know me," Zion grumbled with his eyes still on the beauty who had walked in with his brother.

She was a siren. She stood short at 5'1" with fair, freckled skin, and dark reddish orange hair. Her breasts were small, a mouthful at most, and she had a small waist with wide hips and an ass so big that he could see it from the front.

Zion wasn't sure if it was her sexy body or gorgeous face that had his heart racing. Her slanted, jade green eyes quickly peered around the office, and she frowned. She took a seat on Zion's sofa and began to roll up. She was oblivious to Zion's stare.

"Nigga, you know I ain't got shit to do but work," Zion mumbled, still gazing at the beauty.

Zeke nodded. He walked around his brother's office in deep thought.

"You sure you don't? Last I checked, you had this small ass person waiting at mom's crib for you. Guess you forgot about that," he quipped.

Zion broke his gaze to peer up at his brother. His brother wasn't perfect. He cheated on his soon to be wife every chance he fucking got. Nigga couldn't stay out of the streets for shit, and he was responsible for half of the drug dealings in Michigan. He was the last nigga who should have been looking down on someone.

"You got it, but aye, who this?"

Zeke stopped glaring at Zion to peer at his beautiful lady for the day. He'd been trying to bag her for weeks, and she was giving him the run around, although she never hesitated to let him eat her pussy.

"This is Jordyn. My future wife," he gamed.

Zion chuckled. His brother was a muthafucka. How the fuck was he claiming a bitch when he was already engaged to another one? Cheating had never been Zion's style. He was careful with his dick. He liked to stick it in the same heavenly place. Fucking around with different women caused drama, confusion, and broken hearts. A bunch of shit he didn't have the time or patience to deal with.

"Look at you, nigga. Hey, beautiful, you want something to drink?" Zion asked Jordyn, just having to say something to the sexy lady in his office.

After a few moments of silence, Jordyn looked Zion's way. Her neatly arched brows pulled together, and she quickly shook her head. A frown marred her precious face as she went back to rolling her blunt.

Her attitude was rude as fuck. Zion snarled at the way she'd blown him off. He wasn't used to that.

"Damn, Zeke, I see you entertain snotty bitches now," he commented.

Jordyn smiled to herself.

"Not snotty, just not interested in small talk. Last I checked, I wasn't here to see *you*, nigga."

Zeke chuckled. That was why he fucked with Jordyn. She said whatever she wanted and didn't apologize about it. Women like that always turned him on.

Zion nodded, not amused by her reply. He brushed his hand over his low-cut fade as he stared Jordyn down. His hair was nice. It held a softness to it that he credited his Somalian mother for. She was legit with her beauty. That type of melanin that never aged, and like the loving mother that she was, she'd passed her genes down to her three children.

"Zeke speak before I put you and your uptight bitch the fuck up out of here," Zion replied.

Jordyn waved him off, not caring how he spoke of her. She'd heard worse.

"Aye, Bezo her people, so fall back with all that bitch shit, but I'm stopping by for your daughter. She needs you, nigga. You don't think she's hurting?" Zeke asked.

Zion's nostrils flared. His skin grew hot as he stared at his brother. He felt like Zeke was once again speaking on some shit that didn't concern him.

"You don't think I'm hurting? I lost her too."

Zeke nodded, looking at Zion.

"You didn't take the loss the way she did, though, man. Let's be real about this shit," his brother replied, and Zion sat up in his seat.

"My nigga, I'ma tell you one time to get the fuck out of my face with that bullshit! You gone make me fuck around and beat your ass up in here," Zion warned him.

The growl in Zion's tone was enough to make Jordyn stand and leave his office. Zeke walked to the door and glanced back at his brother. He was hurt that Zion was once again taking his anger out on him.

"I understand you mad, but don't act like you the only one fucked up behind this. You don't owe me nothing, but her, the child you made is the one suffering the most. Think about that while you out here acting like Batman and shit, chasing niggas down. What's gone happen if you catch a hot one? Then she gone be visiting both of y'all grave sites."

Zeke left once he'd said his peace, and Zion stared up at the ceiling. His thoughts went to his daughter. He loved her. His family knew that shit. They also knew that right now he didn't need to be around her. He was fucked up and bringing her into his murky world would only fuck her up too.

CHAPTER

Two

"DAMN," Zeke groaned.

Jordyn lay back with her eyes on the ceiling. Above her bed were sayings she'd written down the first night she moved into her apartment.

You're beautiful!
   Fuck him!
   He doesn't deserve your love!
   Jordyn, you can do this!

. . .

"This pussy taste so fucking good, sexy. Can I stick it in?"

Jordyn's brows furrowed. She quickly sat up and pushed Zeke back. He was cool and all, but she wasn't about to give herself to him. Fuck no! If she was to lose her virginity. it would be to someone she felt something other than lust for.

"Um no, I can't. I told you I'm not cool with that. Sorry," she said in a bland tone and rose off the bed.

Zeke gripped his hard member as he watched her sway her sexy, naked body over to her connected bathroom.

"Baby, you killing a nigga! I won't even finish. Just let me get a few pumps in. We been kicking it for a month, ma," he said and groaned.

Jordyn quickly washed up and stared at herself in the mirror. She pulled her bottom lip into her mouth and exhaled. Her freckled skin was flushed, and her thick lips were swollen from kissing Zeke. Her slanted eyes were red, and her wild curls were all over her head. She wished that the beautiful girl looking back at her was happy.

"Zeke, four weeks isn't shit. The way your phone be going off, I know you have someone else, so let her handle that. I don't wanna have sex anytime soon."

Zeke peered around Jordyn's room and shook his head. Pretty, thick as fuck, and all, she was still turning him off. He was a handsome looking nigga. His mother hadn't only blessed Zion in the looks department; he'd garnered her good genes as well. Zeke kept his hair in a curly taper with a neat lineup. He possessed dark brown skin and was covered in body art. He went hard in the gym, and it showed, not to mention he was always rocking a nice fit. He refused to continually dine and splurge on a bitch who wasn't giving it up.

Nah, he wasn't that nigga.

"Well, this is where we part ways, sexy. When you start busting that shit open, hit me up," he said with no anger in his tone.

It wasn't personal; he just couldn't fuck with it anymore.

Jordyn nodded. She was used to men walking out on her. The only man who had ever held her down was the man her mom was married to.

"I understand. You be good, Zeke," she said, and he appeared in her doorway.

Jordyn gazed up into his light brown eyes, and her heart pumped faster. Zeke was attractive, but she just didn't feel a connection with him. She only felt lust.

"Nah, you be good, baby. And I'm for real. You start fucking, call a nigga," he said and pulled her into a mouthwatering kiss.

One so passionate that it caused Jordyn to moan.

Zeke hit her with his confident smirk before leaving her bathroom. Then, like all the other men who realized they couldn't fuck, he was gone.

"And another one bites the dust," she mumbled.

Jordyn went into her bedroom and turned her Lauryn Hill playlist to one of her favorite songs. She perched herself on her bedroom floor and lit up her joint. Jordyn was twenty, but she housed an old soul. She preferred doobies instead of cigarillos. Old school music instead of new age R&B, and she craved love. The type of love that was so deep the ocean would be jealous. A love that she felt she never had. A love that her young mind wasn't sure existed.

She was lost.

No one looking at her would be able to tell. Jordyn was a model and full-time college student. Her stepdad, the famous rapper, Bezo, footed the bill for her schooling, not wanting her to have college bills while she paid her own rent. Bezo only asked that she get her college degree, and she was two years shy of giving him and her mom her undergraduate degree.

"Can't take my eyes off you. You'd be like heaven to touch. I wanna hold you so much. At long last love has arrived, and I

thank God I'm alive," Jordyn sang, sounding like her favorite singer.

No one knew that she could blow. It was something that she loved and valued so much that she wanted to keep it for herself. Jordyn didn't want the world to change her love for singing. She didn't want it to ever be a burden, especially since she considered it a blessing. To do it and get paid for it wouldn't sit well with her either. Jordyn never wanted to become a slave to her passion.

"Oh, Lauryn, what the fuck am I doing with my life?" she asked aloud as her cellphone began to ring.

By the tone alone, she knew who it was. A smile fell onto her pretty face as she took the call.

"You always call at the right time. What's up with you, pretty girl?" she asked her friend.

Vadah sighed into the phone. They'd met through school and work and were now thick as thieves. It had only been months, but they felt as if they'd known each other a lifetime. They could relate on so many things, and Jordyn liked how transparent Vadah was. With her, what you saw was what you got.

"Nothing. Stressing over these bills. I blew through too much money in Cali, and now my damn car might be re-possessed. I need to book some shit ASAP," she vented.

Jordyn shook her head. Vadah was a full-time college student and modeled on the side like her. Vadah's shopping habits were much worse than Jordyn's, so Jordyn couldn't relate to the going broke one day after being paid thing.

"All that Gucci when they don't even want us wearing that bullshit. You better take that mess back," Jordyn said, making Vadah snicker into the phone.

"Shit, I really need to, though. I spent ten thousand dollars in a day like I'm rich. At the time, I was all in, swiping away. Now, I'm feeling that shit. A bitch don't even have noodles in the cabinet. I'ma call Ace and see if he got something on the floor for me. I'ma be doing shit all month to get out the hole. I saw you and your new boo all over Snapchat too. He's fine as fuck."

Jordyn rolled her eyes at the thought of Zeke. He was cool and always kept grade A weed, but he wasn't a keeper. His impatience to stick around for sex was proof of that.

"He's cool, but you probably won't see him again. I told him I wasn't down with fucking, and he told me to call him when I was. I chucked up the deuces, and he left," she replied.

"Wow. These niggas can't wait for shit. Well, it's definitely his loss. If I was a man, I'd wait for your fine ass. You hanging tonight? You know any club we hit the drinks on somebody's man or daddy," Vadah jested.

Jordyn laughed. Her girl was silly but right at the same damn time. They never had to pay for anything when they went out. It was one of the luxuries that came with being a young, beautiful woman.

"You funny, but nah, I'm good. Zeke topped me off before he left, so I'm tired. Plus, this weed has me high as hell. I'll hit you up later, and if you do go out, be safe. You know niggas is crazy," she told her girl.

"Oh, I know. Love you lots, get some rest," Vadah said and ended the call.

Jordyn smoked on her joint until it was a roach then she placed it in her glass jewelry box with all her other roaches that she smoked on the days when her funds were low. She slid into her comfy bed and eventually dozed off to sleep.

The next day, Jordyn stood in the middle of the studio with her modeling clothes on. She turned slightly to her left, and the cameras flashed. Her head was tilted up with her enchanting light eyes staring at the ceiling as she pushed her round derrière out as far as she could.

"Yes, you killing it! Turn around for me so I can get the back of the shirt, beautiful," the photographer called out.

Jordyn did as instructed, and a few whistles let off as she did so. She rolled her eyes at how immature men could be at times. She wore leggings, but still they acted as if she was nude. She wouldn't dare be on anyone's ad half naked. She had way too many people to answer to, plus, she didn't have to. Jordyn was so beautiful that off her face alone, she sold products.

"Aigh't, we done. I got a few more shoots coming up. You down?"

Jordyn spun around and smoothed down her unruly, silky strands. She prayed the stylist didn't put any chemicals on her natural hair. If so, she was positive she would soon be fucking that bitch up.

"Yeah, as long as I get paid. And I need the contracts sent over to my email. You know how I do," she coolly replied.

The photographer smiled. He admired her beauty as she rushed to the backroom to change. Once she was back in her street clothes, she re-entered the room and was met with fresh faces. One was a man who was so handsome that Jordyn found herself openly staring at him. He was tall with smooth mocha brown skin and inky black hair that was cut into a fade. From his chiseled face, thick lashes, and full brown lips, he rendered Jordyn speechless. He possessed the kind of skin that you wanted to kiss on. There was also a commanding presence to him that grabbed your attention. Jordyn swallowed hard as she found herself openly admiring his good looks.

"You couldn't speak to a nigga before, but now you wanna stare?"

Jordyn's eyes widened. Not only was his question confusing to her his voice was insanely deep and sexy as hell.

"Huh?" she asked stupefied.

Zion chuckled. He looked Jordyn over and licked his full lips. Like before, she looked outlandishly beautiful. The type of beautiful that was rare. The type of beauty that many women paid to possess.

Zion shook his head and Jordyn closed her mouth. Her eyes slid over his dark fit that he'd paired with designer sneakers, and she licked her lips.

He was fine as shit to her.

"Forget I said anything about it. How you like modeling for my company?" he asked, making his photographer smirk at him.

Jordyn shifted from one foot to the other. The man speaking to her did look familiar now that she'd thought about it. Before, she'd been too engrossed in her own thoughts to notice his looks, but now things were different. Jordyn did see him, and *damn*, she couldn't pull her eyes away from his. It was something in his gaze that drew her near. It was like there was an invisible cord tugging Jordyn to him.

Jordyn licked her lips, loving how handsome he was. Shit, he even bordered on being pretty. She was all smiles until Zeke popped into her mind. Her shoulders fell as she thought of all the sinful things, he'd done to her with his tongue.

Great. The one guy that I can't take my eyes off, and his brother just happens to know what my pussy tastes like. Just great, she thought.

"Just email me the details, Leroy," she murmured to the photographer.

Jordyn turned around and briskly exited the studio. As she stepped into the hallway, a firm hand grabbed her arm. Jordyn stopped walking and glanced back at Zion. Her regular mug sat on her face, making him smile. She looked as angry as he felt.

"Slow down, ma. You ran out that muthafucka like the cops was on ya ass," Zion joked.

Jordyn smiled. As much as she wanted to continue to glare at him, she didn't. Zion had a way of breaking the hard resolve that she often carried with her. Her phone started to vibrate as she stared up at Zion.

"I'm sorry. What is it that you want? I have to get to class."

Zion let her arm go and placed his hands in his pockets. His brows pulled together, and he frowned. His russet eyes looked Jordyn over before he shook his head.

"Honestly, I don't know. I'll let you go," he replied before walking off.

His response baffled Jordyn, but she didn't have time to ponder it. If she wanted to become a pharmacist, then her ass had to go to class.

"Smile. You look even more handsome when you do that."

"I am smiling," the man grunted.

Jordyn sat closely behind the couple with her black hood over her head. Not that she felt he would notice her any damn way.

"Rome, please put on a happy face. You'll find another job. The company closing down had nothing to do with you."

Jordyn shook her head. Even after all this time, he was still unstable. He still didn't have his shit together.

Go figure.

"I'm stressed. You know I thought about her again today," Rome gloomily replied.

Jordyn's heart rate increased at his words.

"Did you call Logan? Regardless of your past, they should give you her info," his wife replied.

Rome shook his head.

"Call and say what? I'm your dad, the nigga who stopped being there for you at five. I can't do that. I won't," he said solemnly.

Jordyn's words became lodged in her throat. Her eyes watered, and she quickly rose to her feet. She briskly exited the coffee shop and got into her car. As she started it, her cell rung through her car's Bluetooth.

"Aye, girl, we miss yo ass in the A. When you coming home, sis? You got Mom and Dad all angry around this bitch. Since you left, they won't let me or Toni do shit. You ruined it for all of us by moving out the house," BJ spoke into the phone.

Jordyn smiled. She was six years older than Bellamy Jr., and he was her everything. She loved her hooping, destined for the NBA little brother.

"Aww, shut your crybaby ass up, boy," Jordyn said, and they both laughed.

With ease, she pulled onto Woodward Avenue, headed for the freeway so she could go home.

"I'm far from that, sis. I'm just saying, what the fuck is in Detroit besides Grandma Megan?"

My daddy.

Jordyn shook her head.

"I was tired of Atlanta. I am grown, you know. So, what you all been up to?"

Bellamy Jr. sighed.

"School and working at the cleaners. You know Auntie Kolbee is running the new one, and I be up there with her. That's my girl."

Jordyn snickered.

"That's my girl?" she mimicked him.

It was no secret that Kolbee spoiled Bellamy Jr., and at first, Jordyn was pissed because Kolbee was *her* auntie, but Kolbee had a way of making them feel equally loved. Kolbee didn't play that favoritism shit. She spoiled them all, including Toni, who was the baby of the bunch at ten.

BJ chuckled into the phone.

"You such a fucking hater, sis. But, for real, we been doing us. I was on ESPN again," he said proudly.

Jordyn grinned at her brother's words.

"I know. I was watching. I'm your biggest fan, Bellamy. I always will be," she assured him.

"I know, and I'm yours too. I found your journal the other day. I didn't tell them, I just put it back, but I hate you feel that way. You know Pops loves you with all his heart, Jordyn," he quietly said.

The sadness in his deep tone made Jordyn swallow hard.

"Bellamy. I know he loves me, but the fact remains that he is *your* father and Toni's. Not mine, and he has been great to me. I can't recall him even whooping me. It's just that I've always felt a loss inside of me. I've always wondered what my life would be like had my real father been there for me. I also wonder why he wasn't, you know? Was it something I did? And that's just how I feel, but please don't tell them. They'll force me to come home. Mommy hates him so much. I hear her talking about him all the time to Auntie Jerrica and Auntie Kolbee."

"I won't. I just don't like you out there on some spy kids shit. I know that's your people, but J, if he didn't care back then, what makes you think he cares now?"

Bellamy's questions pierced Jordyn's heart. She licked her chapped lips as she pulled onto the freeway. It was hard to explain to someone who always had their father in their life how it felt to never have your biological dad around.

They simply didn't understand.

"You don't get it, and you won't. You're one of the lucky

few. You have a dad, and he's amazing to you, to all of us. Just let me do me. I'm still in school, and I'm still modeling. I'm still handling business. Make sure you continue to handle yours. Okay?"

Bellamy Jr. chuckled.

"Already done. I love you, and I'm here. Fuck school, fuck ball. None of that matters but family. I'll drop whatever to come to you. Okay?"

Bellamy was so much like his father it was insane. Jordyn smiled at his heartfelt words. Whatever woman he married many years from now would be lucky to have him as her husband.

"I know, and I love you too. I'm only a call away," she responded before ending the call.

Her cell rang again, and she smiled.

"Hey, Granny!"

Megan, her mother's mom, smacked her lips.

"Don't 'hey Granny' me. You been here for three months, and you still haven't come to see me. You need to be driving my way now," she demanded before hanging up.

Jordyn laughed as she changed direction and headed to Redford Township. She knew that if she didn't go to see her granny, a phone call from her parents would soon come.

CHAPTER
Three

"SHE WANTS THAT BIG ONE, *I'm stroking nice and long.*"

Vadah danced to the music despite the ratchet lyrics. Despite the sweat that was sliding down her back, she wined her waist. Despite the ache in her foot due to the uncomfortable heels she wore, she made sure she danced on beat. Vadah felt like she was good at finding the next *it* song, and she knew that Wayne Mack was trash. Still, she did all the things that were expected of her until she felt his large hand grabbing parts of her that wasn't on the menu.

Vadah took a step away from him, and the second verse kicked in.

"*She wants it from the back, lil momma ass so fat. Nigga damn near had a heart attack.*"

Vadah struggled to keep a smile on her face. The lyrics were mediocre, and that was her being nice.

"Dance more up on him, lil momma," Fleetwood directed, making Vadah roll her eyes.

Vadah moved closer to the touchy, feely, rapper and like he'd done seconds before, his large hand fondled her ass again, only this time, he went a step further and pinched it.

Vadah bit the inside of her cheek to hold her tongue. The music began to play again, and she was pulled back onto the handsome but rude rapper's erection. Vadah's cinnamon brown chunky cheeks flushed in anger. Her car note was due. She was $25,000 in credit card debt, and she didn't want to even think about her student loans. She *needed* to finish the video. Her livelihood depended on the money she made from videos, but damn, the rappers were making it hard for her to continue to do so.

"Aye bounce that ass! Quit bullshitting!" the director yelled, growing aggravated with her lack of enthusiasm.

Vadah breathed through her nose as she slowly gyrated her hips. It wasn't long before the rapper pulled her back into him. He swung his arm over her shoulder, and a cocky grin fell onto his face as he cupped her sex aggressively while rapping his vulgar lyrics into the camera.

Vadah's eyes widened in alarm. *Never* had she been forced to deal with so much disrespect. She snatched away from the rapper and glared back at him.

"What the hell is wrong with you? Didn't your mother teach your ugly ass some manners?" she asked, making everyone on set look her way.

"Bitch, what?" he asked, giving her a stupid grin. He was shocked but more embarrassed than anything that Vadah had called him out.

Vadah gave him a once over, and her small, button nose flared in anger.

"You heard me. Don't ever in your sorry ass life touch me like that again. Ain't enough money in the world for me to let you touch on me like that," she replied.

The director looked their way and shook his head. Vadah was a hot commodity on the music scene. All the big-time rappers wanted her. She'd just finished shooting a Future video, so he'd paid top dollar to get her. But where he came from, money was king, and Vadah had to earn that check. He didn't give a damn where the rapper touched her as long as he was able to shoot the video.

"Vadah, what's good? You need a minute to chill out?" he asked, walking over to her.

Vadah rolled her eyes at the director. Since she'd been on set, he'd been letting the rapper disrespect her. It was clear that he wasn't on her side. She needed the money like a muthafucka but refused to sell her soul to get it. She had to stand for something, even if that meant losing out on a check.

"Fuck this, I'm done," she said quietly and quickly walked past the director.

She rushed to put on her clothes and shoes. Models that she'd met over the years gave her empathetic smiles as she pulled up her track pants.

The director along with the up and coming rapper walked over to her. The rapper was the first to speak as he glared at her with his dark eyes.

"So, you one of them stuck up bitches, huh? You trying to front on a nigga 'cause he new to the game? Baby, I been getting money," he said, and his Louisiana twang fell off his tongue naturally as he pulled out a knot of fifties.

Vadah didn't mind going at it with the best of them, but Wayne had chosen to disrespect her on a day that she was just plain old tired. Instead of trading colorful banter with him, she chose to flip him off and exit the studio. Vadah went to her two door Beamer and got in. As she nestled into her seat, her eyes closed.

Vadah could feel her heart thundering in her chest. For two years, she'd been a video vixen. For two years, she'd been a social media celebrity. She was paid to do shows, rock weaves, and show off clothes. In the beginning, it was fun, but the older she got, the more over it she became. She wanted to let go of the modeling and focus on school, but her thirst for shopping was one of the reasons she still held on. It also didn't help that she was living a life that cost a lot of money. She wasn't in a dorm, and she had monthly bills that needed tending to. She could have gone to the mall for a job like some people, but no mall job would be enough to keep her happy. Minimum wage money just wouldn't suffice.

Slowly, she opened her eyes and gazed out of her window. In a city like Detroit that was always alive with people on the go, Vadah felt like she was at a standstill.

"God, I need a new plan. This isn't working for me anymore," she admitted for the first time out loud before starting her car.

After stopping for Chinese takeout, Vadah drove home. She'd chosen to listen to gospel music to lift her spirits. Vadah considered herself an all-around type of girl. She could do trap music at night, pop in the mid-day, and gospel in the morning. For her dispirited mood, only songs about the Lord could lift her spirits. As Tasha Cobbs' "For Your Glory" was going off, Vadah's cellphone started to ring. She looked at her phone and smiled.

"Hi, Momma. How are you doing?"

Vadah's mom, Carmen, coughed into the phone.

"I'm good, baby. I'm getting over a cold. I was calling because I have good news for you," she replied.

Vadah got out of her car with her phone pressed to her ear and rushed into her condo. She went into her bedroom and dropped her food bag onto her black suede duvet.

"And what's that, beautiful? You know I miss you, right?"

Carmen smacked her lips, not buying Vadah's sweet words.

"You haven't been home in weeks. You must not miss me that much, but I have a job for you. A caregiver to a mother of two. I know you said that you're tired of those videos, so why not take this job? Especially since you've dropped your classes for the rest of the semester," her mom said, making her gasp.

Vadah sat on her bed and allowed her Givenchy slides to

fall to the floor. She knew her mom checked her grades online, but damn, her mom wasn't playing games. She'd just dropped the classes, and already, Carmen knew.

"Ma—"

"Don't. I won't judge, but I also won't sit back and continue to watch you use your body for financial gain like you weren't born with a brain. You are so much more than that, Vadah. Have you spoken with your father lately?"

Vadah snorted. Her who? That nigga was everything but her fucking father. More like a sperm donor who she hadn't called daddy since she was a kid.

"Mom, please. Let's keep this conversation on the right track. He chose his mistress. The whore he employed over us, and now he can love her and her kids."

Carmen sighed.

"Oh, honey. Your father cheated on me, not you. I hate that you were even old enough to see me hurting like that because it has changed things for you all, but that was over ten years ago. He loves you, and he wants to get close with you. Give it a shot, but in the meantime, let go of them scummy videos and get your act together. Are you going to take the job?" she asked Vadah.

Vadah swallowed hard. She hated doing videos, but she loved the money.

"I don't know. I'm broke, Ma, and the money is good. I promise, next semester I'll get good grades. I didn't drop my classes because of my job," Vadah replied.

"Vadah, don't bullshit me. I've sat back for two years and watched you do this mess. I'm being too polite, so let me say it in a better way. You're done with those videos. You will take this job, you will get back on track with school, and you will call your father. Or I'ma be on your ass. Okay?" her mom asked in a stern tone.

Vadah recoiled at her moms' words.

"Okay," she muttered, feeling much younger than she was.

"Good, now check your PayPal. I sent you some money to cover your bills. I'm emailing you the details now of the job. This job is easy, and it's safe. You aren't degrading yourself for it. I love you, Vadah, more than you could ever know. As your mom, it will always be my job to make sure you are living your best life. I'll call you tomorrow," her mom said and ended the call.

Seconds later, a PayPal notification came through that made Vadah smile. She looked at the $5,000 and felt the weight on her shoulders get lighter. She could pay off her bills and still have spending money.

"I guess I'll do the job until school starts back, and I get my shit together. No lie, I'ma miss that video money, though," Vadah admitted as she stripped down.

"Talking to yourself again?" Jordyn asked as she stepped into the bedroom.

Vadah looked up at her girl and smiled.

"You know I'm loco. All the women with good pussy is. You ain't know?"

Jordyn smiled as her green eyes stared Vadah's way.

"I guess that explains why I'm so crazy. There was a note on your condo. I think it's another one from your dad, girl," Jordyn said and placed the paper onto Vadah's black dresser.

Vadah put on a robe before sitting on her bed. She opened her food container as she stared at her friend.

"Fuck him. I'm real close to getting a restraining order against his ass," she snarled.

Jordyn shook her head as she joined Vadah on the bed.

"At least he wants to talk to you. My biological dad is too pussy to even reach out to me. He's a bum. You been blowing me up for days talking about we hanging, and you not dressed. Is it because of that shit with old boy?" she asked.

Vadah tore into her food and even passed Jordyn a few

pieces of chicken. She rolled her eyes as she grabbed her water bottle off her dresser.

"He online talking shit already?" she asked, referring to the rapper she'd just gotten into it with.

Jordyn smiled.

"Of course, he is. He's lame as fuck, though. They going in on his ass. Even your male followers are on that nigga's head," Jordyn replied and laughed.

Vadah snickered as she stuffed her face. She'd been through drama before with salty rappers, so she wasn't surprised.

"Anyway, my mom got me a job. You know she has a caregiving business. I just dropped my classes, and her ass knows already. She wants me to stop doing videos, Jordyn."

Jordyn nodded. She looked beautiful as she sat next to Vadah. Her curly hair was in a slick, high bun while she wore a gold cowl neck Versace dress that clung to her thick frame. Jordyn was stacked like she'd spent thousands on it, and Vadah loved everything about her. From her slanted green eyes to her freckled skin and full lips. Jordyn was the truth.

"I think you should as well. The videos will only place a label on you that will take forever for you to get off. Why did you drop your classes?" Jordyn asked.

Vadah shrugged.

"Shit, I was tired. I couldn't tell my mom that, but I party a lot. I be too fucking tired to go to class. I'ma get my shit together, though. And yes, we can still hang. I just need fifty hours to get dressed," Vadah joked and passed Jordyn her food so she could get dressed.

"Tell me why I ran into Zeke's brother at a photoshoot. I guess it was for his company, but anyway, he was fine as hell. Like, Vadah, he was *everything,* and I was gone shoot my shot until I realized who he was. I hate I had to fall back from him," Jordyn said and popped chicken into her mouth.

Vadah smiled as she headed for her closet.

"Technically, you didn't have sex with him, sooo…"

"So, nothing! I can't take it there with him. I am not a hoe," Jordyn said with a mouth full of food.

"I never said you was." Vadah laughed and stepped into her walk-in closet.

She slowly looked through her dresses until she pulled a red Fashion Nova number off the rack. Vadah had thousands of dollars' worth of free clothes that she wore religiously so she could continue to get her sponsor checks from the companies.

Vadah grabbed her sparkly Louboutin's and took a shower. She quickly changed into her outfit for the night and did her makeup in her bathroom. Vadah had a look to her that set her out amongst the crowd. Men often went wild over her cinnamon brown skin, long, inky black hair, and almond shaped hazel eyes. Vadah had the pouty, full lips and the high cheek bones that were every photographer's dream. While her breasts were a succulent b-cup, she possessed thick hips with a round ass and luscious thighs. Her body wasn't exaggerated. It was a real woman's body that was naturally thick in the lower half, and it always got her attention.

Vadah pulled her long hair into a high ponytail once she was finish painting her face. She spritzed herself with some Michael Kors Jasmine perfume and walked back into her bedroom. Jordyn sat on the bed with a small bottle of Patron in her hand as a big smile graced her beautiful face.

"Shots?"

Vadah shrugged. Who didn't need a little tequila in their life?

"Why not? Just a shot, though," she replied, and Jordyn giggled.

"Okay, just a shot."

The line outside the downtown Detroit club was so long that Vadah knew if it hadn't been for her status she wouldn't have stayed because she didn't do lines. Because she and her friend often hosted parties there, they were able to skip the line and were given a booth and a complimentary bottle of champagne by the party promoters. Vadah and Jordyn danced in their sections, feeling good off the liquor.

"Hey, gorgeous, can we get some pictures? My boy up in here, and he's a big fan," a security guard said, walking up to Vadah.

Vadah looked past the burly man, and her eyes zeroed in on the booth next to her. Tall, attractive, men of different shades and all in immaculate shape filled up the space. Their tables were covered with bottles while the strong stench of weed escaped their area. Vadah didn't even know you could smoke in the club, yet there they were, openly blowing blunts back.

What caught her eye was the tall man with penny hued brown skin who couldn't take his eyes off her. Vadah immediately knew who he was. Quan was an NBA legend. One of the reasons the Detroit Pistons cut up the way they did in the league. He was talented, and everyone had dubbed him a young Mauri, who was also an NBA legend. Vadah blushed, shocked to see someone of his stature vying for her attention.

"Not Quan, I'm talking 'bout the nigga next to him," the guard said and laughed.

Vadah burned with embarrassment, and the guard laughed harder. She shook her head as her eyes rolled.

"I'm good," she said snidely and turned her back to him.

"Can I get a pic then? Y'all can come chill with us," Chauncey, another NBA baller, said as he walked up to Vadah.

Vadah shook her head, and Jordyn smiled at the handsome baller.

"We'd love that. Is that Cali shit y'all smoking?" Jordyn asked.

Vadah smiled at her pothead friend and followed her along with the man to his section of the club. They all took a seat, and Vadah tried to ignore the sexy ball player, Quan. His presence was commanding as he sat beside her slouched on the sofa. His tall frame took up a lot of space as he bopped his head to the music while holding a drink. Eventually, he finished his drink and pulled his phone out. He sat up and watched old highlight reels of an NBA game as the party went on around him.

Vadah wasn't sure what it was, but she couldn't take her eyes off him. His penny toned skin was heavily tatted. She could see the body art climbing out of the opening of his black collared shirt. He wore slacks with Louboutin loafers, and in a club filled with men wearing street gear, he stood out.

Vadah felt like his boys had swag, but it was nothing in comparison to Quan. His demeanor alone dripped with authority. The way his broad shoulders flexed when he held his phone made Vadah's panties wet then there were his looks.

His hair was cut low to his head in a ceaser while a well-groomed mustache and goatee sat on his handsome face. His eyes were hooded with an amber glow to them.

Eyes like a wolf, Vadah thought.

Vadah sat up to make a drink to ease her nerves, and it was as if Quan was noticing her for the first time. Those amber eyes of his softened when they landed on her.

Vadah stared back at him and noticed that his eyes pulled her in like a beacon. The longer he stared, the more she felt her nerves take over her body. After a few minutes, he smiled at her and sat back. The game still played on his phone as he dropped it into his lap.

A lap that she felt *any* woman would have loved to sit on, including her.

"You want another drink?" Vadah finally asked, wanting to say something to break the staring contest they were having.

Quan glanced down at the phone before looking back at her.

"I mean this with all respect, Vadah, but how did you get into our section?"

Vadah's eyes immediately darted over to his boy, who was trying to finesse the panties off Jordyn until something dawned on her. Quan had called her by name. She looked at him and smiled widely, showing him the deep dimples that she possessed.

"You know me?" she asked.

Quan smirked at her before glancing back down at his phone. His eyes, those enchanting amber peepers, looked her way, and he shook his head.

"You'd know if I knew you. I know *of* you. You've hosted at a few of my clubs and shit like that." Quan stopped talking and glanced back down at the phone again.

"Aye, Quan, it's at capacity. We had to turn a few actors away, and they were talking shit. Just giving you a heads up," a young man dressed in a black two-piece suit walked up and said.

Quan's handsome face frowned as he looked up at the man speaking to him.

"Fuck 'em. Capacity is capacity. Fuck them niggas gone chill at, the ceiling? You know I don't do no ass kissing, so them complaining don't mean shit to me. Whining ass celebrities," Quan replied like he wasn't a celebrity himself.

The young man chuckled before walking away.

Vadah watched him grab the bottle of champagne that was in front of him and take it to the head. She knew she was being creepy, but she couldn't turn her head.

"You gone stare at me all night?"

Vadah watched his lips move, and he chuckled. He passed her his phone, and she looked down at the wide screen. The phone was luxurious, and Vadah had never seen a phone like it. She saw the symbol at the bottom of it, and her brows furrowed.

"Lamborghini makes phones?"

Quan leaned toward her, and she was awarded his panty dropping scent. It was mellow with the right notes to it that made her want to bask in the smell of it. She struggled to not sniff him as he tapped the screen on his phone.

"Yeah," Quan said in almost a grunt while watching the game on his phone that sat on her lap.

Vadah used the moment to look at him even more closely, and she noticed that he had two letters tattooed behind his ear. She eyed the diamond that stuck out of his ear as his eyes peered up at her watching him.

Vadah's cheeks flushed.

She'd been caught.

"Was you sniffing me?" he asked.

Vadah quickly shook her head and he chuckled.

"I'm just fucking with you. What you think about my team? I've seen you courtside at my games with that lame ass nigga who can't get in a good movie for shit. He probably begging the illuminati to take him in, so they can revive his career."

Vadah couldn't help but laugh at what he'd said about her fake boyfriend. Many people would have figured they were a couple. She had gone to all social events with him for the last year and had even vacationed with him, but it was all for show. He was gay, and she was his beard. He'd paid her well to look pretty on his arm, but over time, she'd gained a friendship with him and stopped taking the money.

"It's not like that," she said quickly, making Quan frown at her.

He sat back and nodded, seeming to know what she meant without her having to say it.

"I figured it wasn't. He doesn't know shit about being

with someone like you. Plus, you have that look," Quan said and smiled.

Vadah exhaled as she smiled back at him.

"What look?"

Quan grabbed his phone and paused the game. He stroked the bottom of his goatee for a moment before smirking at her.

"Forget I said that. I saw how hype you be at the games, so I know you love the sport. What you think about my last game?" he asked.

Vadah looked at him for a moment, praying her honesty didn't offend him.

"They were cheating really bad that game. And y'all defense team has really been slacking lately," she expressed, throwing in her two cents.

Quan looked back down at his phone and nodded.

"I was just thinking the same thing. Any more tips you got for me?"

Vadah swallowed hard. Just talking to him made her nervous.

"Well, you could throw to Kris more in the first quarter. Lately, you've been burning yourself out quick by trying to make all the points. You have a good team behind you. Why not take advantage of them? Why do you insist on playing in every quarter and making every shot? Plus, no one likes a ball hog," Vadah replied.

Quan stared at her for a moment. His thick brows pulled into an intense frown. No one had ever spoken to him that way. The coach, his team, even his family told him to keep up the good work. Quan sat up, and a chuckle fell from his full lips. He started to laugh, and everyone in the area took notice. They couldn't remember the last time he'd done such a thing. A few stragglers even took photos, looking to sell a fake story. This was the NBA king Quan with the new music video queen Vadah. Whether the story they told was true or not, people knew it would sell.

"Aye..." Quan cleared his throat. He leaned closer to Vadah so she could hear him. "I'm not a ball hog. They just always toss the shit to me. Fuck I'm supposed to do?" he asked and gently tapped her leg.

Vadah shrugged. His simple touch sent her body into overdrive.

"I don't know," she mumbled, too spellbound to say anything else.

"So, who should I be worried about?" he asked, staring at her.

Vadah sighed. She cleared her throat as she tried to get her shit together.

"Oklahoma and the Warriors, but you know that already, and maybe the Lakers since they have my man playing for them."

Quan sat back with his eyes still on her.

"Your man, huh? Yeah, okay." He chuckled lowly. "That's what's up. I'll keep that in mind, Vadah."

With that, he turned his attention to his boy next to him, and Vadah got up from her seat to join Jordyn on the other side of the section.

Jordyn looked at her and shook her head.

"He's fine. I think he's with his baby momma though," she commented.

Vadah nodded. She had no clue he even had kids because Quan's personal life had been hidden from the public.

"We were just talking about sports, but I can't lie. It felt good to be around his fine ass. I'm focusing on me, so I'm not on that anyway, but if I was, I would be all over him," she said, making herself and Jordyn laugh.

CHAPTER
Four

"HOW THIS DICK FEEL TO YOU?" his deep voice asked as his heart raced.

The petite girl moaned. Her body was thrown into a position she'd never been in while Zion relentlessly pounded into her. He was in a zone. One that often calmed him until it was done, then his mind was back on revenge.

"*Oohhhhh*, daddy. This pussy loves you," she purred out sexily in her light voice.

Zion swallowed hard. His hand clamped down gently on her neck as he drove his penis in and out of the woman. The louder she moaned, the harder he fucked her. There were many things that he was great at, and fucking had to be near the top of the list. It came natural to him.

Zion closed his eyes. He envisioned the beauty who had been on his brother's arm, and then at his dispensary's photo shoot, and his balls tightened. She was so sexy with her pouty ass lips that he couldn't stop thinking about. Zion envisioned her under him, taking the dick down, and his body shuddered.

"Oh shit," he mumbled, and his companion for the night smiled with glee.

Zion pictured Jordyn staring up at him with her engrossing jade green eyes, and he shot off into his condom. *"Fuck,"* he said in a manly moan.

Zion carefully pulled himself out of the woman and fell onto his back. His date, a pretty business owner who he'd been sexing for a while, stared at him. Even before the tragedy, she'd known him. So naturally, when the act took place, she reached out to him. His dick called her back, and like that, a sexual relationship began.

"I have to fly to Miami for a conference," she said, breaking the silence.

Zion nodded. He sat up, and she stared at his back. The writing, the tattoo describing his pain was all too real.

Lord, why is it that I go through so much pain?

All I saw was black, all I felt was rain

The words seemed to bounce off his golden-brown skin. She'd asked him one time where he'd gotten the troubled words from, and in a grunt, he'd replied, "X." Later, Armani discovered it was a DMX prayer off his first cd.

"That's what's up," Zion said, rising off the bed.

Armani watched his perfect body stand and slowly go into the hotel bathroom. She ran her hand through her sweaty brown strands.

"I want you to come. I was bringing my son, and I thought maybe you could bring your daughter."

Zion shut the door and took a shower. He exited the bathroom twenty minutes later with a towel wrapped around his narrow waist. Armani sat in her same spot, only her laptop decorated her bare lap. Like him, she was about her business.

"Did you hear me, Zion? I think Zory would like my son."

Zion put on his clothes and grabbed his car keys off the dresser. He looked at Armani and cleared his throat. His brooding eyes held a bit of anger in them that worried Armani. She knew it didn't take much for Zion to cut you off.

"Somewhere between sucking and fucking, the lines got

blurred, sweetie. I know you run shit in your life, but Zory is all me. I don't require you to think when you with me. All I need is some pussy. Have a safe flight to Miami," he said before exiting the hotel room.

Zion got into his truck and sparked up a blunt. He loved weed. It was his main reason for opening his dispensaries. What people didn't know was that he grew his own weed. His granny had taught him how when he was fifteen. He knew how to dip it, make it pure, even lace it, but at all his stores, he only did that raw, natural shit. It sold like crack, and it was legit. He owned four in Michigan, two in Atlanta, and three in California. California was where his biggest grow house was, and his sister managed those dispensaries with his close guidance.

Zion had a damn near perfect business life, but his personal life was in shambles. For him, the saying was true.

You simply couldn't have it all.

After leaving the hotel in Southfield, Zion found himself outside of his mother's large home. The first thing Zion did along with the help of his two siblings was purchase his mother a home in the University District of Detroit. Zion sat in his truck as his thoughts drifted to Zory. It felt as if it had been an eternity since he'd last been in her presence. He missed her laugh and her bubbly personality. He especially missed how she effortlessly made him smile.

And like God was taunting him, Zory emerged from the vast, four floor home with his mom, Una, in tow. Una immediately spotted his truck and openly stared at him with sad eyes. Zion watched his mother's silent plea for him to come over, and it tore at his heart strings.

His heart pumped faster as he pondered what to do. His hands began to sweat, and his vision blurred. Zory looked just like *her*. Same cinnamon shaded brown skin with the same pretty, oval shaped face. Zion rubbed at his nose as his eyes watered.

He couldn't do it.

He wouldn't.

He just wasn't ready yet.

His eyes shot to the sky as he started his truck. He licked his lips before speaking.

"I'm sorry, Yana. I'm not ready," he spoke sadly before driving away.

His mom dropped her head as she watched his truck pull away from her home.

Hours later, when the sun went down, and the city's nightlife came alive, Zion sat in his black '96 Impala SS. His black hood sat over his head as his cousin lit a blunt.

"How shit been hanging?" Quan lowly asked.

Zion sighed. Quan was like an older brother to him. Quan, like Zion, had chosen a better route for his life than drug dealing. He was an NBA player who hated the limelight but loved to play ball, so he dealt with it. Zion loved how his cousin was still real. He wasn't fake with his shit, and since everything had gone down in his life, Quan had been by his side. Quan never switched shit up, and that was why he fucked with him.

"I got a name," Zion replied while picking at the leather on his middle console.

Quan nodded. He hit the blunt a few times before passing it over to Zion.

"What is it, nigga? Don't keep me waiting," Quan replied, and Zion shook his head while smirking.

Quan could be an asshole like him at times.

"Some nigga name Tye or Tyshawn from Southwest. You heard of him?"

Quan frowned. He pulled on the bottom of his chin hairs as he looked out of the car window.

"Nah, I haven't. I'll holla at my people and see what they know. Have you been to see her?" he asked.

Zion toked on the blunt, ignoring his question, and Quan glanced over at him.

"You know I would never steer you wrong, right?" his cousin asked.

Zion blew smoke out of his mouth and cleared his throat. He fucked with Quan, but another lecture he could do without.

"Let me be, nigga. How Tamm doing?" Zion asked, changing the subject.

Quan sat back and shook his head while frowning. Zion wasn't trying to upset him, but he saw that his question had done just that.

"She's okay, I guess. She been on some other shit lately, so I been giving her space. I ain't really trying to talk 'bout that shit right now. What I can say is that she gone make it. That's what I know," Quan adamantly said.

Zion nodded.

"She definitely is, nigga. I wasn't bringing that up to make you mad and shit," Zion replied.

Quan nodded.

"I know you wasn't, nigga. The other night at my club, I seen this bad lil broad. She had me wanting to take her ass home and shit, she was so fine," Quan admitted, and Zion chuckled.

"Nigga, since Tamm, your ass been laying low. She must have been the shit for you to want her. How she look?" he asked as his eyes skated across the street to the shiny white Lexus.

He'd been waiting on it for an hour, and finally, the nigga was pulling up.

"She's short with a nice lil body on her. Her face is pretty as shit, and she got some dimples that had me wanting to kiss on her sexy ass. She had some nice ass skin too. She was dressed flashy as fuck, though, and you know I don't like that hoodrat attire. That shit don't move me. I need a woman, not some hoe looking for attention," Quan replied.

Zion opened his mouth to speak until the woman who emerged from the white Lexus with Rick made him snarl. He pushed his door open before he could think about what he was doing, and he angrily trudged over to the car.

CHAPTER
Five

WHY DID *I come here with this corny ass dude?*

Jordyn glanced out of the window before looking back at her Rick, dude for the night. He'd been on her since meeting her at a modeling hair show that he'd funded. He was funny and liked to eat, which was her favorite thing to do, so she entertained him. But now, as she listened to him go on and on about how much he wanted to fuck her, she felt her like for him dissipating.

"You just so fucking sexy, ma. You a nice look for a nigga and shit," Rick said, opening his car door.

Jordyn rolled her eyes as she emerged from the ride with him. She tugged at her green mini dress before looking up. The tall, angry man decked out in all black made her gasp in fear and take a step back.

"Rick, you said you only throw events. I don't date thugs," she said, unsure of what was happening.

Rick, too shook to glance back at Jordyn, shook his head.

"I don't know who the fuck this nigga is. Just stay calm and give him whatever he asks for," he replied, mad that he'd been caught slipping.

Jordyn glared at Rick because of his weak ass response.

"Man, all I got is a hundred dollars on me and whatever she got on her," Rick said, holding his hands up in the air.

Zion looked at Rick and smiled before turning his attention to Jordyn. He walked over to her and grabbed her hand.

"*No*," Jordyn gritted as he started to pull her away.

Worriedly, she peered over at Rick, and he shrugged.

"Man, I ain't know she was taken," Rick said with his hands still in the air.

Jordyn's eyes widened at the nerve of Rick when Zion glanced back at her.

"Relax. I won't hurt you, and it's clear this ain't the nigga you need to be chilling with any fucking way," he said, and led her away from the Lexus.

Rick stood by quietly with his hands still in the air as he watched Zion open his back door for Jordyn. Zion then got into his Impala and pulled away. Jordyn sat quietly in the seat as Quan peered back at her.

"What up?" he asked coolly with his eyes quickly scanning over her sexy frame.

Jordyn shyly waved. With so much uncertainty about what was happening, she was choosing to remain calm for the moment.

What's happening? Am I being kidnapped? And why is Quan here? How does he know this nigga? she wondered.

"You good? Why you hanging around with jack boys, ma?" Quan asked, breaking Jordyn from her thoughts.

Jordyn stared at him blankly before scowling. If they were going to take her, that would be one thing, but to question her moves had her heated. She was grown and damn sure wasn't looking to answer to some nigga she didn't know. She didn't give a damn how big of a celebrity he was. It was bad enough she'd been stuck with Rick for hours that she couldn't get back, and now she was with Zion, and him demanding she come with him had her confused.

What was his angle?

Why did he continue to find a way into her life, and why did it make her heart race at unnatural levels? she wondered.

"I didn't know he was one, but who the fuck are *you* to question me? Just because you're a ball player, that doesn't mean shit to me. You in here ducked off in a raggedy ass car dressed in all black, looking like a *jack boy* yourself," she retorted with her lip snarled.

Quan glanced over at Zion, and they both chuckled.

"Aye, nigga, she is not nice at night," he replied, making Jordyn roll her eyes. "So, that nigga didn't put up a fight, huh? He looked like he was five seconds away from shitting on himself with his fucking hands in the air like you had pulled a gun out on his ass."

Zion shook his head at his cousins' words.

"Shit, he was. He was so shook that he started talking about the money he had on him. I'll get at that nigga another time. I'm trying to see why this muthafucka in the back can't sit her ass still," he replied.

Jordyn's brows pinched together. She was so upset that she was positive her skin was darkening by the second. She balled up her fist as she glared at Zion.

"I don't even fucking know you, so don't make it seem like I'm a problem for you. You didn't have to rescue me, and I wasn't looking for you to. I'm curious as to why you took me with you in the first fucking place, nigga," she snapped.

Quan glanced back at Jordyn, and his intense amber eyes made Jordyn shift in her seat.

"Is there a problem?" she asked.

Quan shook his head with his brows knit.

"Not for me. I do think you should be showing my cousin some respect, though. Rick got so many people gunning for him, you lucky he took you with us. Riding around with that hot ass nigga can't be good for your health, so you really should be thanking Zion instead of talking all that shit," he replied.

Jordyn rolled her eyes, and Zion glanced in the backseat at her.

"Yeah, she seems to be good at talking shit. I'ma take you back to the crib, though," Zion said, making Quan smirk at him.

"Bet. I guess I'll fuck with yo' old, friendly ass later then," he replied, already knowing what time it was.

"Whatever, nigga," Zion said and turned the radio on.

Bezo's latest hit started to play on the radio, and Quan rapped to it. Jordyn didn't speak on her stepfather's song playing, so Zion didn't either.

As Zion pulled up to his cousin's downtown Birmingham townhome, his cousin glanced over at him.

"Let me kick it with you outside of the car, nigga," Quan said and opened the door.

Zion threw the car in park and got out of the Impala. Quan pulled out his cellphone and house keys as he stared at Zion.

"I know how hard this shit has hit you, nigga. That's why when you called and said you was about to find the niggas that did it, I said okay, knowing that neither of us has done shit like this before. We both putting a lot on the line, but still I'm riding with you, because I don't want your ass out here by yourself. But I'm starting to worry now. Zeke hit me up saying that you haven't seen Zory in a while, and you losing it. Jigga even called and said he was worried 'bout your ass. I was feeling like they was exaggerating but I see what the fuck they was saying now. You gotta slow down. For your daughter if nothing else, and what's up with you snatching bitches up off the street?" his cousin asked.

Zion took a deep breath and exhaled. His strong hand brushed over his soft, curly hair that was in slight need of a cut, and he cleared his throat.

"I appreciate you, nigga. Just know that, but I'm not looking for guidance or acceptance on what I'm doing, and that shit with old girl in the car is nothing. I'm just looking out for her."

Quan tossed his keys in the air and caught them.

"Since when your mean ass start being so kind, though?"

Zion smirked at his cousin, not bothering to respond to his question. They dapped each other up, and Quan walked toward his home.

"Stay safe, 'cause I know you don't give a fuck about dying, but *we* can't take losing you," his cousin said over his shoulder.

"Don't worry about me. I'm good, nigga," Zion replied as he walked back to his car.

He got in and glanced over at Jordyn, who was now sitting in the passenger's seat of his ride with an adorable pout on her pretty face. Zion licked his lips as he drove off.

"You good?"

Jordyn smacked her lips and glared over at him.

"I'm fine. Can you stop fucking asking me that? Damn," she grumbled.

Zion nodded and turned his music up. Jordyn was fine, but the last thing he planned to do was kiss her ass. Instead, he rapped along to the songs that played while thinking of Rick and how he really needed to holler at him.

Twenty minutes went by and he pulled up to his dispensary in Plymouth. He put in the code to pull in through the back and parked next to his truck.

"Just so you know, I'm far from a jack boy. I got two degrees and run my own businesses," Zion said, looking Jordyn's way.

Jordyn looked at him and playfully clapped her hands.

"Good for you. Can I go now? Since you kidnapped me and all."

Zion smiled at her feistiness.

The way it stretched his handsome face made Jordyn swallow hard. He was just so damn cute. A definite pretty boy, and she knew he probably hated the term, but that was what he was. From his creamy golden skin to his thick eyebrows and long lashes, she admired all the delicate features on him. Then there was his beard and chiseled jaw that let you know he was all man. Even his adam's apple was appealing to Jordyn.

Zion pulled off his hoodie and Jordyn had to force herself to not ogle the muscles on his arms or moan at the alluring cologne that wafted off his skin.

"Why you always talking so slick? Your attitude can't be that fucked up, ma. I'm not gone believe that shit," Zion said and pulled out a blunt.

Jordyn's eyes widened at the sight of it, and she licked her lips.

"I'm not mean," she replied, still staring at his blunt.

Zion chuckled as his eyes did their own inventory of Jordyn. She was wearing the fuck out of her tiny dress and making his dick hard at just the sight of her in it. He cleared his throat as his eyes landed on her beautiful face.

"You look nice," he told her as he lit the weed.

Jordyn smiled. Her light cheeks reddening under his intense appraisal. She slipped off her Giuseppe's and got comfortable in her seat. As she thought of just who Zion was, she laughed to herself.

"I promise you I'm not a hoe. I don't even have sex," she clarified for him.

Zion licked his lips and nodded.

"I know. My brother was pissed you wouldn't give it up to him."

Jordyn shook her head. She was itching to get her hands on his weed. It smelled like it was A-1.

"I'm sure he was. So, is that why you're all up on me?"

Zion looked her in the eyes, and slowly, he nodded. She was too beautiful to ignore, and he was too real to beat around the bush.

"Yeah, but it had nothing to do with you not wanting to fuck. On some for real shit, from the minute I saw you in my office, you been on my mind. I gotta admit you are one of a kind, baby. Had a nigga searching for you online on some high school shit," he admitted before chuckling.

Jordyn blushed harder. Zion was honest, and she liked that.

"Did you find out anything about me?"

Zion passed Jordyn the blunt and continued to stare at her.

"Yeah, a lot, actually. You a year younger than me. Your pops is one solid ass nigga. I met him a few times at some concerts, and you model, but we can all see you were born to do that. I can't say it enough, ma, you're beautiful as hell," he admitted.

Jordyn hit the blunt with her eyes watering. She wished she felt that way.

"Please stop that. Now, tell me about yourself. Because all I see right now is that you like to chase after women who don't want Zeke."

Zion brushed off her comment to not discuss her beauty, and he looked straight ahead. The troubled aura that surrounded Jordyn pulled Zion in. He surmised that it was because he was a troubled soul as well.

"Shit, I'm a simple man. I run my businesses, and that's it. I used to travel and shit like that, but I stay local now. Got a lot of shit on my plate."

Jordyn grinned over at him.

"Like stalking people in the middle of the night, huh?"

Zion chuckled.

"That was personal. That's not who I am, though. I'm a dad and..." Zion stopped talking when his thoughts drifted to Zory.

Jordyn passed him the blunt and turned on some music. She was battling a storm inside of her also, and she knew the look that covered Zion's face all too well. She rubbed his exposed arm as she searched for the old school R&B station that she loved to listen to.

"It's fine. You don't have to talk about it. But if you did, I could be a good listener."

Zion cleared his throat, and his eyes ventured her way.

"You talk then I will. Deal?"

Jordyn winked at him.

"Clever, but how about we just listen to some music? The right song could speak to your soul and shit. I love *real* music," she replied.

Jordyn found Maxwell's soulful voice, and she sighed. The strong weed Zion had was already beginning to relax her body. It calmed her spirit and allowed her to take a break. Escape reality and float on the wave that the high provided. Jordyn pulled her hair from the sleek ponytail it was in, and she fingered it before allowing it to fall past her shoulders.

Her tongue felt heavy, however. Sitting beside Zion had her antsier than she would typically be off weed. She knew the marijuana wasn't laced because she'd unfortunately had some of that shit before. Jordyn just knew that it was the man who called himself Zion who had her on edge. For reasons unknown to her, she felt the need to talk to him.

"I'm from Detroit. I was born at the Henry Ford hospital off West Grand Boulevard. My mom said it was on the prettiest Monday in May that she'd ever seen," Jordyn said and smiled.

Zion blew smoke from between his full lips.

"I'm sure it was. I was probably outside that day grinning and shit," he replied, making her laugh.

Jordyn rubbed at her arms that had goosebumps.

"I'm sure you were, but my mom moved us to Atlanta when I was younger. I honestly don't have much recollection of living here. No real memories of my father. So, um yeah, I'm back here modeling and in school. I have two more years to go, then I have to go back to school for four more, all so I can become a pharmacist. Yay me," she said quietly with a fake smile gracing her face.

Zion took another hit off his blunt and passed it back to her. Smoke fell from his lips as he exhaled. His eyes peered over intently at Jordyn, and she felt burned by his gaze. She couldn't think of anyone ever staring at her in such a way.

It really was like he could see through to her soul, and it frightened her. However, Jordyn was a thrill seeker, and shit like that, she ran toward.

"Smart and beautiful. You like the whole package and shit. Still, you sound angry, and you always frowning. What would put a smile on your face, Jordyn?"

Hugging my dad.

Hearing him say I love you.

Jordyn shrugged.

"I don't know. I haven't been happy for a while now. It's like I woke up one day, and I was depressed. I don't talk about it, though. My family is good to me. My stepdad is amazing, and my mom is the shit. I feel bad for complaining. I don't want them to be hurt by it, so I keep it to myself. This is my get up, you know?"

Zion nodded. For that reason alone, he had been shying away from his daughter.

"Nah, I get it. You don't want them to be tainted by your bullshit, right?"

Jordyn glanced over at him and nodded. A tear escaped her eyes, and Zion quickly brushed it away. He cupped her face, and she breathed harder. As Zion leaned toward Jordyn, he thought of his brother. He wasn't trying to be on some snake shit, but Jordyn was different. He felt a connection with her that had sparked his interest. He wanted to be around her, and he wasn't about to allow his *engaged* brother to ruin that.

"But you are. You beautiful as fuck, and I hate that you don't see that shit, baby," he whispered.

Jordyn closed her eyes. His words stung when they should have felt like sweet licks against her skin.

"Do you tell your daughter how beautiful she is?" she asked quietly, knowing how every girl needed to hear those words from her father.

Zion stalled. *Damn,* she had him.

"Uh… nah. I don't… I haven't in a while. I don't see her. Her mom was killed along with her boyfriend. My daughter was shot too, but she survived. I haven't been around her since her mom's funeral," he admitted.

Jordyn looked at him. Her eyes, those amazing colored peepers stared at him intensely. He was expecting judgment, but he saw none. She grabbed his hand and pulled his face closer to hers.

"I'm sorry," she whispered before pressing her lips against his.

Zion took control of the kiss and used his hand to slightly tilt her head back. His tongue explored her mouth slowly, eliciting moans with every stroke while his hands gently pressed into her tender skin.

Jordyn moaned and started to suck on his bottom lip. Zion felt the urge to slip his hand into her underwear, and he pulled back. If she wasn't having sex, then he saw no reason to get both of them worked up.

"My bad," he said and pushed the car door open.

Jordyn touched her racing heart and cleared her throat. Damn, he was a good ass kisser.

She exited the car and found Zion walking over to his truck. He opened the door for her, and she thanked him before climbing in. Once Zion was in, he started it and glanced over at her.

"Where you stay?"

"Huh?" she asked with her mind still on the kiss that he'd given her.

Zion smiled.

"Where you stay, baby?"

Jordyn laughed nervously. She looked out of her window then back at him. She felt so comfortable around him and wasn't ready for their time together to end.

"I could go back to your place," she nervously suggested.

Zion raised his brows. Jordyn's response was everything *but* appealing to him.

"You always fuck with random niggas and shit?"

Jordyn rolled her eyes.

"I'm not having sex with them," she quickly replied.

Zion nodded and cleared his throat.

"Letting them lick on that lil pussy is still sex, baby. You need to slow your ass down. Cool off that snatch, momma. You can still catch shit through oral sex," he told her.

Jordyn laughed before glaring over at him. She wanted companionship from men. She *craved* it. She didn't need to open her legs to get it. But she did like to be in the company of a man who wanted her. She'd always been like that and wasn't going to let Zion talk down on her for it.

"Don't judge me. I didn't do you like that, so don't do me. I live in Ypsilanti, and the next time you see me, turn the other fucking way."

Zion groaned, *hating* the way Jordyn popped off at the mouth.

"One minute I'm turned on by you, then you start talking, and the shit leaves. Why the fuck is your attitude so bad? All I tried to do was hit you with some real shit. I know your father wouldn't want you out here hugging up with every nigga that shows your ass some attention. You gotta do better, my baby. That shit is not a good look. You don't wanna be known as the pretty ass hoe."

Jordyn's skin darkened at his words. *My father? Pretty ass hoe?* She turned to Zion, and with strength that she didn't know she possessed, slapped the taste out of his mouth. Zion swerved the truck before quickly pulling over to the side of the road. Before he could talk, Jordyn attacked him like he was out to take something from her.

"You don't know shit about me! Don't speak on my father, nigga! Who the fuck do you think you are?" she yelled while punching him in the face and arms.

Zion took her licks until she calmed down. He then drove off, and instead of taking her to Ypsilanti, he took her to his home in West Bloomfield. He pulled into the driveway and left her in his Maserati Levante truck. Jordyn sat in his ride until she had to pee. She then went into the large, modern style home and shut the front door.

Zion's two-story home was clean and smelled of weed and fresh linen. Jordyn found the downstairs bathroom and quickly used it before finding Zion upstairs in his bedroom. He sat on the edge of his large bed in his black Ethika boxers and with a white hand towel on his head. Jordyn had cut the fuck out of his face with her red stiletto nails.

"You lucky as fuck I had just smoked, or I swear I would have busted your shit open. Don't ever hit no man unless you woman enough to get your ass hit back. Don't try that hoe shit on me again," he warned her.

Jordyn slipped off her shoes then pulled off her dress. She wore her blush pink lace underwear and an apologetic look on her pretty face as she stood in his bedroom.

"I'm sorry. I don't usually act like that," she said, feeling ashamed of her actions.

Zion waved her off, and she went over to him. Jordyn grabbed the wet rag and gently pressed it against his skin.

"You got issues, shorty," he noted quietly.

Jordyn smiled.

"I know, and so do you," she told him.

Zion nodded. He looked up at her and swallowed hard. He was a little angry that even after her attack on him, she still looked like the prettiest woman he'd ever seen.

"We two fucked up individuals, huh?" he asked and touched her hip.

Jordyn slowly nodded. She removed the rag, and Zion pulled her onto his lap. He gazed up at her face as his hands went to her ass.

"Tell me you're beautiful, Jordyn," he demanded.

Jordyn shook her head.

"I don't have self-esteem issues," she let him know.

Zion squeezed her cottony soft ass while he gazed up at her.

"I know. You got daddy issues," he said in a matter of fact way, and it hit him.

Years from now, Zory would be Jordyn. Sitting on a man's lap, needing reassurance that he hadn't given her. Zion coughed and broke his gaze from Jordyn.

Jordyn leaned into him and rested her head on his shoulder.

"It's not too late for her," she quietly told him.

Jordyn didn't know the complete backstory, but what she did know was that every little girl wanted her father in her life no matter the circumstances.

"But I don't know what to say, ma," Zion confessed with his heart racing.

Jordyn pulled back to look at him and licked her lips. She'd never felt so exposed in her life, but it didn't scare her. Zion gave her the effect that the weed did times a thousand.

"How about I love you? Those words can change a girl's life," she said before kissing him again.

"A FEW THINGS you should know. At the last minute, she requested you to stay in the estate. She has an immaculate home that has a guest house. That would be your living quarters. If you were in school, I would have never agreed to it, but this will be good for you. It will give you time to calm down. Give the clubs a break," Carmen told her.

Vadah sat in her car so angry she could scream.

"Mom, I didn't sign up for this. Why the hell do I need to live with this woman? I'm not a nurse. I can't give her medication and stuff."

"First off, you will calm your ass down. I never said you had to do any of that. She will have her own nurse on staff. She has two kids that you will be tending to."

Vadah laughed before shaking her head. Shit was getting worse by the second.

"So, what I'm saying is that you will be like a sitter for the kids. Or live in nanny as you could say," her mom replied.

Vadah bit her tongue to stop herself from saying something that she would later regret.

Live in nanny? What the fuck? She hadn't signed up for any of that bullshit. Her mom was a headstrong woman like herself, and she knew that her mom wouldn't let her walk away from the job without a fight, but still, she was pissed at her.

"Wow, I honestly don't know what to say. I fell asleep a model and woke up a nanny," she quipped sarcastically.

Carmen snorted.

"Vadah, you're finding a safe way to take care of yourself. It's nothing wrong with that. Like I said, if you had been taking your classes, then I would have chosen someone else for the job, but you're not. Suck it up and put on a big smile. FYI, this is the ex-girlfriend of basketball star SaQuan Smith. She sent over NDAs that I signed for you. No one is to know her home's address or about her health condition, not even your pretty friend, Jordyn. Her kids should also stay off your social media pages. They are very private with their business. Okay?"

The mention of Quan nearly made Vadah crash her vehicle on the freeway. She already felt like she'd been driving forever, and now she knew why. She was going to a celebrity's home. They always stayed deep in the suburbs.

"Wow, this is too much," Vadah admitted.

"You'll be fine. Call me if you need me for anything. I've spoken with this young lady several times, and she's adamant on having a young, energetic woman to handle her kids. She's very down to earth. I gotta go, but I'll call later to check on you," she replied and ended the call.

Vadah shook her head, still shocked by her mom's revelation. She would not only be a nanny, but it would be to Quan's kids. She'd been thinking about him for weeks and was rendered speechless at how this crazy scenario had come about. It was so random and a little scary. She vibed out to Meghan Trainor and allowed her soulful, raspy voice to take her away as she drove to her destination.

It wasn't long before Vadah pulled up to the 40,000 sq. ft estate that sat off Walnut Lake Road. Vadah used the gate code her mother sent over to get in, and she slowly drove up the winding driveway.

Because she was a video model, she'd partied with the best of them, but *never* had she seen such a beautiful home. Mansion was the correct title for it, but even with its grand size, it had a homely feel to it.

Vadah pulled up to what she assumed was the garage doors and parked. She stared out of her window and took in the outside décor. The home was white with large pillars near the front door. The yard was done to perfection with beautiful flowers lining the yard. Two golf carts sat in the driveway while a white Rolls Royce Wraith sat near the front door.

Vadah took a deep breath and exhaled. She hadn't been nervous until now.

"You can do this," she said shakily and exited her car.

She walked up to the front door and rang the bell twice. Minutes later, a beautiful woman with *cafe au lait* hued skin opened the door. She wore a white blouse with black pants and a flowery Chanel scarf over her head. She smiled at Vadah as she stood in front of her.

"Vadah Clement?" her light voice asked.

Vadah nodded with a nervous smile on her face.

"Yes," she said quietly.

The woman gave her a warm smile as she looked her over.

"You are beautiful. Hopefully, what I've been looking for. Please come in, Vadah," she replied and walked off.

Vadah frowned, not sure how to respond, so instead, she walked into the home and followed the woman to a well decorated family room. It was vast with an open floor space. Large bay windows with white leather décor and big bins filled with toys. Vadah set her purse down as she gazed at the family photos. She saw the kids along with the woman and Quan. In the photos, they looked like the perfect couple, and it made her feel bad for lusting over the taken man.

"First, let me introduce myself. I'm Tamara, but everyone

calls me Tamm. Five years ago, I was diagnosed with breast cancer. I took chemo, and it was effective. It went into remission and it came back two years later. I did another round, and it was again successful. However, it's back again, and it's in the fourth stage, Vadah. In between all of that happening, I split up from my children's father. You know him as Quan, but to me, he's just SaQuan. We met when we were kids.

"We had our first child at sixteen, so yes, I have a nine-year-old running around here. Her name is Morgan, and she's a diva to say it mildly, but we love her abundantly. Six months ago, I had another kid for him. *Only* for him because I didn't think we could handle two but yet our Ace still made a way into this world. I've been too sick to even take care of him so it's been a struggle," Tamm said and her light eyes watered.

Vadah found herself getting emotional at the woman's story.

"Like I told the owner, who I also know is your mom, I would like this to stay between us. With the NDA that you signed, if any of our business was to leak, you all would be sued. SaQuan is very private with his family. He doesn't like for us to be photo'd in any way. You didn't even know about me or his kids, did you?" she asked.

Vadah laughed.

"No, I didn't. My friend told me about you, but that was it. I think that's a good thing. My whole life is on the internet," Vadah replied and shook her head.

Tamm smiled as she stared at her.

"You should take down those pages for your time with us. Would you mind doing that?" she asked.

Vadah internally groaned. She couldn't fucking live without Instagram. Slowly, she nodded, and Tamm smiled wide.

"Also, please keep the titties covered. I'm far from jealous, it's just that SaQuan is old school. He likes for women to be modest in public and freaky behind closed doors. A fucking caveman, but he's a good man. So, you will need to stay here with us Monday through Friday and some weekends. I can't stress enough to you how private we are. No one must know about my health, my kids, or my home. Okay?" Tamm asked.

Vadah nodded, feeling overwhelmed by the job. Tamm smiled again as she looked at her.

"Great. I'll need your bank info, so we can set that up. Weekly, you will receive $1,500. We will cover all food, gas, and living costs while you are with us. We take care of the people we love very well. Your mom also spoke of your college debt. I'd like to handle that bill for you as well," Tamm told her and walked off.

Vadah stood in shock. So many things were happening, and she wasn't sure how to act or what to say. It was like she was in a dream. It just didn't seem real.

"Will chemo keep you sick?" Vadah asked as she trailed behind Tamm.

They went into another living room. One with a more formal feel, and Vadah noticed the expensive leather furniture and exquisite wall art.

Tamm sat down on the loveseat and patted the spot beside her. Vadah sat down, and Tamm grabbed her hand.

"Chemo is draining me. I've done it twice, and I can't put my family through that again. Cancer has taken so much from me, but this last time will be my choice. I'm choosing to spend these last few months with my family, and I'm not going to do that while being sick. I won't let their last memory of me be that. I need you to help me do that. I feel like you're the one. You could be what I've been searching for," Tamm replied.

Vadah struggled to hold in her tears. She wasn't sure what to say. Tamm spoke so highly of her, and she didn't know why.

"I don't know if this job is for me, honestly. You seem so

excited to have me, and I'm scared because I don't want to disappoint you," Vadah admitted.

Tamm laughed.

"I'll explain more later. Let me show you to your living quarters. Your only job will be to help with the kids and their daddy. I know you've met him. I saw pictures of you two online at a club a few weeks ago."

Vadah swallowed hard.

"I was just there with my best friend. I'm not like how the media says I am," Vadah assured her.

Tamm shook her head.

"It's fine. I only love him as a friend and the father of my kids. With he and I, that ship has sailed, Vadah."

Vadah nodded as she walked beside her. She was trying to process everything while also keeping her cool.

"Your place for now is this way. The job is for six months, but we may need you longer. If so, I will pull up another contract when the time comes, and if for any reason you have to stop working with us, just let me know. Don't be afraid to say it," Tamm told her.

Vadah nodded.

"Okay," she murmured.

"By the way, I love your look. Every time SaQuan is watching one of your videos, I smile. You're just so pretty, a real natural beauty. Kind of reminds me of the girl off that show *Star*. I think her name is Ryan Destiny," Tamm said while smiling.

Vadah smiled as they passed through the gorgeous stainless-steel kitchen. People often told her she looked like a thicker version of the actress, and she sort of agreed with them. As they stepped through the patio doors, it took them into a massive backyard. It not only had a guest house but also a tennis court along with an infinity pool.

"Thank you. Coming from you, I'm truly honored. You're

super fine yourself, while you playing," Vadah said and meant what she said.

Tamm laughed lightly.

"I used to be before cancer came into my life, and please call me Tamm. You're a part of this family now. Do you need anything before I lay down for my nap?" Tamm asked, opening the guest house door for her.

Vadah shook her head as Tamm's older sister walked up with a frown on her face. She'd been known for dating a few ball players, and Vadah knew because of the media that she was going through a nasty divorce.

"Tamm, I'm not done talking with you! Don't ignore my fucking phone calls!" she said.

Tamm pointed to Vadah while smiling.

"This is Vadah. She's going to be here for a while, so get used to seeing her face. I'm having her pick the kids up for me today, so you don't have to," Tamm replied.

Vadah smiled wide at Tamm's sister, and the sister rolled her eyes. She stared at Tamm for a moment before turning around and walking the other way. Tamm shrugged as she led Vadah into the guest house.

"I just told my family today about my decision to let chemo go. So, you have to ignore her anger. It's misplaced. Um, anything you do concerning the kids is done in the Jag truck. The tint is dark, and the kids' car seats are already in there. The instructions on where to go and how to pick them up are on your dresser. Do you have any questions?"

Vadah shook her head, although she had a million questions swirling through her mind. Tamm smiled and pulled Vadah into a hug.

"Perfect. I'm so happy you're here. It's God sent," Tamm expressed before leaving the guest house.

Vadah stood in the middle of the floor for a moment, still in shock. Slowly, she walked around her temporary home, admiring the cozy décor. Once she was done inspecting the place, she called her mom.

"I know you have questions, but I just have to ask you mine first. Is she nice to you, and do you feel like you can do the job?" Carmen asked.

Vadah cleared her throat.

"Mommy, why did I take this job? This is pretty much an everything job. She has me washing clothes, picking up her kids, and I have to cook. I can't do all of that," Vadah vented.

She'd read over the papers on her dresser, and her eyes had widened at all the things that were expected of her.

"Honey, she is willing to pay off your student loans on top of paying you good money. This is a good job, and I don't want you to let it go. At least give it a week. Okay?"

Vadah pouted. This was really more than she'd bargained for.

"Okay," she mumbled.

"I just know that you'll like it in no time. I have to run some errands, so I'll talk to you later."

Vadah ended the call with her mother and replied to a text that she had from Jordyn.

Jordyn: *how is it? I need deets!!!*

Vadah: *It's okay. Too much shit to text. I'll call you later. I have to delete my social media pages FYI just letting you know so you don't think I blocked you. It's for work.*

Vadah then deleted her pages and made a quick run to her condo for clothes before going back to the estate. It wasn't long before she had to grab the kids from school and daycare. She grabbed the keys to the truck Tamm left for her and walked out of the guest house. As she was walking around the home, she spotted Tamm having a heated discussion with Quan and her sister. They all stared her way from the patio, and she quickly walked off.

Vadah got into the stark white truck and pulled out of the driveway. She used her GPS once again to get to Ace's daycare, and she parked near the front of the building. Vadah walked in and was greeted by the front desk receptionist.

"Hi, I'm here to get Ace Smith," she said with a smile.

The front desk receptionist nodded.

"I'll just need to see your license, and you also have to take a photo for your lanyard," she replied.

Vadah nodded, and after they were squared away with the photo, Ace was brought out. Vadah immediately smiled as she was handed over the chunky, tawny brown skinned, handsome little boy who looked like the splitting image of his father.

"Hi baby!" she gushed as she held him.

He smiled like he'd known her his whole life as he grabbed a piece of her long hair.

"He likes you already. Tamara said you were coming, so we've been talking to him about you," the daycare worker said, staring at Ace.

"Well, I adore him already," Vadah said and ruffled Ace's long, soft, curly black hair.

Vadah said goodbye to the daycare workers and left the business. She carefully put the baby into his car seat and used the GPS to get to Morgan's school.

"Damn, all these people up here already," Vadah grumbled while pulling into the school's pick-up line as Tamm had instructed on the papers.

Vadah sat inside the truck for ten minutes, and soon, kids spilled out of the large elementary school. The back door was then pulled open, and a mini Tamm slipped inside the truck. The pretty brown skinned girl with hair so long it hung past the middle of her back stared Vadah's way.

"Who are you?" she asked angrily.

Vadah smiled. She began to pull off after waving to the teacher who had already been notified of who she was.

"I'm Vadah. Your new babysitter, you could say," she replied politely.

Morgan frowned as she put her seatbelt on.

"You put his belt on too tight. He can't breathe, and you can call me Miss Morgan," the girl let her know.

Vadah rolled her eyes.

"*Okay*, I'll call you by your first name, nothing more. And, trust me, he's good. How was school?"

Morgan rolled her eyes. She pulled out her headphones and glared at Vadah.

"Don't talk to me. We are not friends," Morgan replied and began to play music on her iPhone

Vadah cleared her throat to keep her cool.

"She's a kid. Just let her little spoiled ass make it," Vadah said lowly.

"And I only eat Chick-Fil-A," Morgan said, not bothering to look up at Vadah.

Vadah nodded as her words went in one ear and out the other.

"Whatever, lil girl," Vadah murmured and turned the radio up.

Vadah eventually made it back to the estate, and before she could fully park, Morgan was out of the car. Vadah watched Morgan run into the home while she struggled to carry Ace and hold his bag. As she walked into the estate, she bumped into Quan. He wore black Nike workout clothing with a small frown on his handsome face. His amber shaded eyes looked her over briefly, and he gave her a small nod before he grabbed his son. Vadah's heartbeat increased as she peered up at him.

"You don't have to carry him. Let his fat ass crawl until he's ready to walk. He on his way to it, shit," he grumbled while holding his son.

Vadah watched Quan drop to the ground and begin to play with his son, all while making Ace laugh his heart out. She smiled at the scene before moving past them and going into the kitchen. She set Ace's bag onto the island and sighed.

Tamm's sister, Tera, stood near the island with a drink in her hand. When her eyes connected with Vadah's, she scowled at her.

"I'm not my sister, so don't get it fucking twisted. You are *not* a part of this family. You're the help. Quan, nor these kids, nor this home belongs to you, and it never will. It already has a lady of the house. Don't forget your place, lil girl, or I will remind you," she sternly told Vadah and left the kitchen.

"Okay, this is too much. I can't deal with bitches' moods, misplaced or not," Vadah said as she walked to the sink.

She quickly washed her hands and picked up the recipe book that Tamm had waiting for her in the kitchen. Vadah chose to make lasagna with salad and garlic bread. She hummed to herself as she quickly made the dinner. Vadah actually loved to cook but never had the time because of her hectic schedule.

An hour later, she was preparing to set the table as Quan and his teammate stepped into the kitchen.

"Damn, shit smells good. Who this?" his teammate asked, smiling at Vadah.

Vadah wiped the sweat from her brow as she looked at Quan and his friend. Her hair was sweated out. Her clothes were wrinkled, and she was tired as shit. All she wanted to do was go to bed, and her day wasn't even over yet. She still had to tend to Ace and help Morgan with her homework. All of that had her second-guessing things. She still wasn't 100% sold on if she could do the job.

"Well, you can eat if you want," she offered as Quan watched her intently.

He was now dressed in blue AMIRI jeans that he'd paired with a white crew neck and blue and white limited-edition Jordan's. In his hand was a Hermes carryall that matched the color of his jeans.

He was as handsome as he'd been the last time, she'd seen him, and Vadah had to force herself to not ogle him. The cologne he wore was placing a spell on her that she couldn't fight.

"I'm headed out of town, but I left all my numbers on your bed. I had no clue that you did shit like this, but it's a better look than them bullshit videos. Meet me in the hallway real quick," he said and walked away without waiting for a response.

Vadah ignored the jab about her change of profession as she followed him. She met Quan in the hallway and watched him brush his left hand over his low-cut taper. His amber eyes stared down at her as he licked his lips.

"Regardless of what Tamm told you, she's gonna make it. My kids are my world. I don't play that dumb shit when it comes to them. No social media, no friends over here, and especially no niggas. *Ever.* If you need anything, call me, and *always* pick up when I call you. I don't live here, so when I get back, you and the kids will be coming to my place for a while. Okay?"

Vadah shook her head. It was all too much to process.

"I didn't sign up for this. I had no clue I would have to stay with you as well," she said quietly. "That won't work," she told him, not ready for anything of that nature.

Quan nodded. His eyes looked past Vadah, and she glanced back to see what he was staring at. Her eyes connected with Tamm's, and Tamm waved at them before walking off.

"I'll just stay here then. You should get Ace from her. She never complains, but it's hard for her to have him for long periods of time. She's in pain, ma. You good?" he asked.

Vadah nodded, although she was everything but good.

"I guess." She sighed.

Quan rubbed her arm, and she held her breath. His touch made her heart race. He leaned down and moved some of her straight strands behind her ear.

"Relax. Ace likes you already, and Morgan soon will too.

Call me if you need me, and I left some money on the bed for you. I'm gone," he said and tapped her hip before walking off.

Vadah stood in the hallway stuck until she heard Ace's piercing cry. And like she'd been doing for years, her instincts kicked in, and she headed for Tamm's room to grab him. She planned to quickly tend to the kids so she could lie down and process everything that had happened to her that day.

CHAPTER
Seven

"YOUR GRADES LOOK GOOD, but I would rather see your pretty face. How have you been?"

Jordyn stopped talking with her mom to peer over at Zion. He was walking around his warehouse checking on his plants with his two workers who were in charge of growing them by his side. His business was set up nicely, and Jordyn was impressed with how professional everything was. It wasn't some trap house get up. Zion had a big ass barn that was top of the line for his marijuana plants, and everything was up to code.

It also didn't hurt that he looked good as hell on any day of the week. He'd told her that it was a dress down day for them, yet he still wore nice threads. Phillip Plein jeans with black Yeezy's and a black polo. On his head was a Detroit snapback while wired Cartier frames covered his eyes. Jordyn had seen a lot of men in her young life but none of them had ever affected her like Zion had.

"I've been great, Momma. I miss you all so much!"

Jordyn's over enthusiastic voice made Zion glance her way. It had only been a month, and already they were learning each other in ways that no one else knew about.

"I'm sure you do. So, who have you been hanging with? Momma said you rarely see her, and Jerricka said she can never get you to answer the phone," her mom replied.

Jordyn's eyes roamed over to Zion, and she smiled.

"I've been hanging with Vadah," she said, telling half the truth.

Vadah had been working her new job as a nanny while Jordyn had been up under Zion, but they did find time to catch up on the phone at least once a week.

"Oh, I love Vadah. How is she? What have you two been doing?"

Jordyn sighed. Her mom could be pushy at times.

"We've been doing modeling gigs and going to class. That's about it, ma."

"Mmhmm. Well, why haven't you been posting pics with her? You've been with some boy. I saw his shadow in one of your snapchat videos," her mom replied.

Jordyn could only smile at her mother's detective skills.

"You are so beautiful, ma. How is Toni doing?" she asked, referring to her younger sister.

"She's great. Missing you like the rest of us. You would tell me if you weren't okay, wouldn't you?" her mother, Logan, asked, turning serious.

Jordyn swallowed the lump in her throat.

"Yes, I swear I would. I'm truly fine out here," Jordyn promised.

Her mother sighed with relief.

"Good, now who is the boy on your Snaps?" she asked again.

Jordyn cleared her throat. Her mom was relentless with her questioning.

"I have a friend," she quietly admitted.

Her mom laughed.

"I know you do. You're beautiful like your momma. I'm

sure they're all trying to be your friend. How is this friend treating my baby, and what the hell is his name?"

He's been giving me booty rubs that would make any bitch jealous. Oh, and he's been giving me pussy massages too. My God, they feel so good!

Jordyn smiled to herself.

"His name is Zion. He's a year older than me, and he owns his own business. He's really sweet, and he treats me good."

Logan was quiet for a moment before sighing.

"That's good. That's what he should be doing. Jordyn, two things before I get off this phone. One, your dad wants to meet with you for lunch, so go to your granny's today at five to meet up with him. Two, I'm coming home this weekend. I know what you're doing, and I want you to stop. Sometimes we can go searching for things that aren't there. We have to accept the things that we can't change, sweetie. I love you, I miss you, and I'm here for you. We are all here for you. You're always going to be my princess Elsa-Ana-Jordyn," her mom said, making her smile.

Jordyn laughed at the nickname she'd given herself as a child and was surprised to see her mom still remembered it.

"I love you too, Mommy," she whispered before ending the call.

She checked the time as Zion walked up behind her.

In just a brief period of time, they'd become each other's medicine. With Jordyn around, Zion didn't have the intense urge to seek revenge. With Zion around, Jordyn didn't stalk her biological father, Rome.

For now, it worked for them. They were sprung and finding it hard to go one day without seeing each other.

"You ready?" he asked, hugging her tightly.

Jordyn sighed. His scent was so fucking calming.

"Yes, I have to go to my granny's to meet up with my stepdad. You will have to take me back to my car."

Zion's brows pulled together at her words.

"Or I could go with you," he suggested.

Jordyn looked at him with a smile on her pretty face.

"Or you could go see Zory," she rebutted.

Zion let her go and slapped her ass.

"I'll take you back to your car, but call me as soon as you're done," he replied.

Jordyn shook her head, wishing he would have chosen the latter. But two weeks into seeing him, they made a promise to not judge each other, so she was trying to uphold her end. However, Zion was making it hard. He was a good man, and she hated that he only provided financially for his daughter who she'd seen from pictures looked exactly like him.

"We'll see. I might have a date," she joked.

Zion scooped Jordyn up and spun her around in a circle, making her laugh.

"Yeah, date my ass. If you wanna go out on a date, all you gotta do is let a nigga know."

Jordyn stopped laughing as he set her down.

"Or you could just surprise me. I am getting tired of all of them damn takeout meals we been knocking down. I'm gaining weight all in my face and shit," she complained.

Zion smacked her ass again, which had also gotten bigger.

"I see it's going here too. I like that." He grinned before they walked out of his warehouse.

Beside Zion's truck was a sleek, red Mercedes coupe. Zeke leaned against the car with his fiancée, Dream, by his side. Zion slowed his steps as his eyes connected with his brother's.

"Damn, what's up? I had to pop up on your ass just to see your face. And who is this you got with you?" Zeke asked with his nostrils flaring.

Jordyn, never the one to bite her tongue, smiled at him. She walked over to Dream and shook her head as she eyed the pricy engagement ring that sat on her slender finger.

Zeke's fiancée was a beauty, and Jordyn couldn't understand why he was cheating on someone as gorgeous as her.

"I didn't know he was engaged, and just to get it out there now, he did eat me out. That was before I met Zion, though. If you all could please excuse us, I really have to go," Jordyn said and walked away.

Zion chuckled while shaking his head as Dream turned to a stunned Zeke.

"It was a joke, damn!" Zeke yelled as he snatched an angry Dream up.

Zion and Jordyn got into his truck, and Zion glanced over at Jordyn.

"You don't have no fucking filter, ma. You didn't have to do all of that," he told her.

Jordyn put on her seat belt and shrugged.

"I figured I would say it now to clear the air. Then he wouldn't be able to have that over either of us, and she would know from the jump that I'm not the wrong party. It's him. Plus, I like you. I didn't want that shit with Zeke to cause friction with whatever this is that we have going on," Jordyn admitted.

Zion nodded with a smirk on his handsome face. He pulled away from his warehouse and glanced over at Jordyn. She sat beside him in skinny black jeans with a white cropped top and Allure Boutique slides. Her hair was in six long, feed-in braids, and she wore minimal makeup that gave him a front row show of her freckles.

"I like the way you think, and just so you know, if he does come at you on some fuck shit, I'll handle it. I see you're aggressive, and that's cool, but I'm wearing the pants round this bitch, baby," he replied.

Zion took Jordyn back to her car and gave her a sensual kiss before pulling away. Jordyn collected herself then drove to her granny's. As she pulled up, so did her stepfather, Bezo. Bezo had come into her life at a time when she was questioning just where her biological father was. Jordyn loved Bezo and appreciated everything that he had ever done for her.

She parked her car and quickly got out. Bezo emerged from his black Range Rover all smiles. He didn't care about that biological shit. To him, Jordyn was his child. He'd been there for her when she'd needed to learn how to rollerblade. He was the man who made sure no ghosts were in her closet, and he was the only person escorting her to the daddy, daughter dances. Jordyn taught him how to be a father, and he was slightly hurt by how she was playing shit now that she was back in Detroit. On some days, Jordyn wouldn't even take his calls, and that hurt because he loved her as if she was his own biological child.

"There she goes. I see your phone is still working for your mom," Bezo said as he walked over to Jordyn.

Jordyn's pretty face stretched into a smile. Her stepdad still dressed as if he was in his early twenties, and it worked for him. He would never be caught dead in shit like skinny jeans, but he still rocked his snapbacks, chains, and sneakers. He didn't look like he was someone old trying to be young; he simply looked like himself. She gave him a quick hug before they got into his truck. Bezo started up the Range Rover and headed to the restaurant. Jordyn's granny was gone gambling, and her home was merely the meet up spot.

"Talk to me, J," he said, breaking the silence.

Jordyn glanced over at her stepdad as he rode down the street. To many women, he was the insanely sexy rapper with the unique style and good looks. To her mother, he was her loving husband, and to Jordyn and her siblings, he was just their dad. Bezo *never* treated her any different from Bellamy Jr or her baby sister, Toni, but still, she felt it.

Jordyn didn't start to feel the disconnect until she was twelve. She'd watched her childhood friend deal with her parents divorcing, and it made her really think about Rome.

That was when Jordyn's interest in her father heightened, and from there, it had only progressed.

"What is there to say, Bellamy?"

Bezo shook his head. Sometimes she called him dad. When she was younger, she did it all the time, now she only did it sporadically.

"Somethings going on. Me and your mom can both feel it. Don't bullshit with me, Jordyn. Regardless of how you feel, I do know you," he stressed.

Jordyn tossed her arms over each other and gazed out of the window.

"Maybe I'm looking for my dad," she mumbled.

Bezo nodded with his eyes on the road.

"And how is that working out for you?"

"I know where he's at. I just haven't spoken to him."

Bezo's jaw tensed at her responses.

"Shouldn't he be tracking you down, though? Why the fuck should you have to look for him?" he asked.

Jordyn's hands balled into a fist.

"You don't understand. He's my daddy."

Bezo pulled up to the restaurant in Dearborn and parked in an available spot. He shut off the car and glanced over at Jordyn. His eyes held a look of hurt as he stared Jordyn's way.

"He is? It takes much more than making a kid to be a parent. What has he done that makes him your father?"

Jordyn rolled her eyes, and Bezo rubbed the waves on his head. He was blunt, but it was always out of love.

"I'll never sugar coat this for you. I know how your mom is. She's soft with you and your siblings. I understand why she's that way, but I can only be me. I don't wanna see you get yourself hurt. You could be chasing some shit that's gonna break your heart, baby girl."

Jordyn took a deep breath and exhaled.

"What if my heart is already broken?"

Her question angered Bezo even more.

"Then we try to find the best way to heal it. Let's go eat," he said, and they exited the truck.

After signing a few autographs, Bezo and Jordyn were shown a table in the back of the steakhouse restaurant. Jordyn responded to a few texts from Zion while Bezo watched her closely.

"You need to come home. I don't have a good feeling about you being here, Jordyn. We can come back later to pack your shit."

Bezo's words made Jordyn look up from her phone. She stopped smiling as their drinks and breadsticks were brought out.

"I'm grown. Daddy don't do this," she whined.

Bezo shook his head while smiling.

"Don't give me that look. I don't like this shit, and your mom doesn't either. I'll never throw dirt on your pops' name to you, but he isn't the guy you think he is. I know he isn't."

Jordyn looked at Bezo and narrowed her eyes.

"How do you know that?"

Bezo stared back at Jordyn, not backing down from her intense stare.

"Because if he was a different man, he would be here. He wouldn't let pride or none of that shit stop him from being in his daughter's life. Instead, he's not, and that tells me all I need to know. I never had my dad in my life, J. I didn't know shit about a father figure until your grandpa Deron cane around. He showed me how it was to have a strong man in my life. With you and your siblings, I just do my best. I know I'm not perfect, but I love y'all. You are my daughter, Jordyn. It's not nothing I wouldn't do for you," he told her sincerely.

The look Bezo gave Jordyn was the reason why Jordyn had been so hushed about her feelings. Her emotions were being transferred to her family, people she cared about, and that was the last thing she wanted to happen. Just because she was hurting, they would now hurt too, and it made Jordyn feel guilty.

"You are, and you always will be. It's not anything you or mom did wrong," she assured him.

Bezo sighed. He tossed back his drink before looking back at Jordyn.

"But how can I fix it?"

Jordyn smiled. Just for that question alone, she would always love him.

"It's not up to you to fix. This problem is something I have to handle, Daddy," she replied while looking his way.

Bezo broke the gaze. He glanced around the restaurant before peering back at her.

"Who is this lil nigga you been texting?"

Jordyn's eyes widened.

"What?" she asked innocently.

Bezo waved her off while chuckling.

"You heard what I said. Who is he, and is he good to you?"

Jordyn thought of Zion, and she smiled.

"He's a really good man. You would like him," she replied with a look on her face that made Bezo suck his teeth.

"I wanna know everything about him, starting with his full fucking name, baby girl."

"So, how did you meet him?"

As promised, Jordyn's mom came into town and brought with her, Jordyn's younger sister, Toni. While Toni watched YouTube on her phone, Jordyn and her mom cooked in the kitchen that she rarely used. Jordyn knew it wasn't healthy but spending a weekend without Zion was driving her insane. He'd been texting her around the clock, basically counting down the time until they would be together again.

"He owns a clothing line, and I modeled some of his clothes, ma," she replied while admiring her mom's good looks.

Jordyn's mother, Logan, was a looker. Average height with flawless brown skin and red hair that always brought attention to her. It wasn't dyed, and people often fawned over it. Jordyn's mom and aunt had been born with the ginger hued strands, all thanks to her grandfather, Deron, who had passed years ago.

"I love that he's a business owner. What's he like?" her mom asked with a smile.

Jordyn shrugged, feeling her cheeks darken.

"He's laidback like me. We both like old school music, and we love to eat. He's cool, and he's cute. He's Black and Somalian," Jordyn proudly replied.

Logan nodded while staring at Jordyn.

"I'm sure he's very handsome. Have you been to see Rome?" her mom asked as Jordyn stirred the cake batter in the big, yellow bowl.

Jordyn shook her head while avoiding eye contact with her mom. Her mother walked over to her and pulled her by her side. Her mom's floral scent covered the space around them as Jordyn's eyes watered.

"When I got here, I went by every place that I thought he would be. I found his address and stopped by his home. His wife told me that he was out of town for business. I don't know if I believe her, but she said that he would call me when he got back. Regardless if he calls or not you will be okay, Jordyn. You don't need his love to survive," her mom said in a low tone.

Jordyn nodded. She blinked, and her tears began to cascade down her face. Her mom took the bowl from her and placed it on the counter. She then pulled Jordyn into a hug and rubbed her back. Jordyn cried softly as her mother held her.

"But do you think he will call?" she asked and sniffled.

Her mother sighed before shaking her head.

"I don't know, baby. I really don't know," she replied, and Jordyn hugged her tighter.

CHAPTER
Eight

"THIS IS UGLY, and I'm not wearing it! I want my momma!" Morgan yelled at the top of her lungs.

Vadah sat at the edge of the bed with Ace on her lap. High end bags covered the floor in the suite while Morgan threw a fit. Vadah was at odds on what to do. She wasn't around kids often, so she didn't know how to handle Morgan's unruly attitude. She felt that Morgan looked cute in her black dress with her colorful tights and her Valentino flats.

Morgan, however, hated the look.

"I want my momma!" Morgan yelled again, and tears slipped from her brown eyes.

Ace started to cry, and somehow, Vadah's own tears started to fall. Vadah was so stressed that she could have pulled her own hair out. Quan walked into the room wearing a navy two piece Dolce & Gabanna custom suit with black shoes. He looked at the three-crying people in front of him, and he chuckled. His tapered fade had been freshly cut with his beard perfectly trimmed. His Louis Vuitton Ombre Nomad cologne wafted around the room, and his presence alone seemed to immediately calm everyone down.

"Morgan, go wipe your face, then you coming back to

apologize to Vadah, or you won't be watching the game from the floor seats. Now go," he told her, and Morgan moved like she had ants in her pants.

Quan then grabbed Ace and sat him in his play pen. He gave him some baby finger food to suck on before turning his attention to Vadah.

"You let them pull your card, ma?" Quan asked, and Vadah smiled weakly as a few more tears fell.

"I'm just overwhelmed. Plus, I'm worried about this game. You have been playing kind of shitty lately," Vadah replied, making Quan chuckle.

He smirked while looking down at her.

"They got you emotional *and* delusional. You look too nice to be so sad. Come here, Coach V," he said and wiped her face with a napkin.

Quan helped her stand up, and his amber eyes gave her a deliberate once over. With the help of Tamm's stylist, Vadah was dressed in designer from head to toe. She'd always worn nice clothing, but her outfit for the night was on another level. It was high fashion and a huge difference from what she was used to.

Her hair had been silk pressed and parted down the middle as she wore natural looking makeup with bold, red lips. Her lash extensions were dramatic, as a peach jumpsuit from a Paris designer covered her thick frame. She wanted the latex dress the designer had brought into the suite, but one look from the demanding Quan, and she changed her mind. On her feet was a pair of six-inch Giuseppe's, and while she wanted to rock flats because she had Ace, she refused to. This would be Quan's kids' first time attending his game, and she knew they would make the papers. She refused to be in pictures at a game wearing some bullshit ass flats.

"All of this is for Morgan, right?" she asked playfully with watery eyes.

Quan continued to stare down at her. He nodded as he

took a step closer. His big hands went into her hair, and he fixed her diamond drop earring that had gotten tangled in her inky blueish black strands.

"Yeah, all of this is for her. I'm sure Tamm told you this before we left, but no talking to reporters. Let them think what they want. This is my business. Fuck them. Okay?"

Vadah nodded.

"Okay," she murmured, lost in his amber gaze.

Quan smirked at her before licking his lips.

"You can't let them run the show. You have to be stern with them and show them who is boss. Morgan will get you every time if you let her. I have to leave now, but my security will take you all down in an hour. I have headphones for Ace because it will be loud in there. After the game is over, we hopping right back on the jet. I'm trying to get Tamm to go to this appointment tomorrow," he replied before leaving the room.

Vadah sat on the bed and glanced over at Ace. She'd been doing the job now for over a month and was still getting used to it. Ace was getting better with each day, however, Morgan refused to listen to her and was making her job as hard as it could possibly be.

"Let me call up Jordyn real quick to see what her ass been up to," she said and pulled out her phone.

Vadah smiled at Ace as she called her friend. Jordyn answered the call seconds later with Lauryn Hill playing in the background.

"I miss you so much, housewife! How is it in Orlando?" Jordyn asked and coughed into the phone.

Ace began to whine as he stared at Vadah, and she rushed to pick him up. Instantly, he calmed down and rested his head on her shoulder. He hugged her tightly as she walked back over to the bed.

"Orlando is cool. I'm tired as hell," Vadah admitted.

Morgan stepped into the room with wet eyes. She looked

at Vadah and rolled them before going over to the extra bed. Vadah cleared her throat as she rocked Ace to sleep.

"But how are things going with you?"

"So good. Me and Zion are actually chilling right now. Do you think you can do six months of this job? It seems like it's stressful," Jordyn replied.

Vadah had to laugh. Her friend had no clue just how stressful her job was, but it was rewarding also. She'd grown close to Ace and even Morgan. She was building a bond with Tamm and was still shamefully lusting over Quan. She felt bad for wanting him in such a way, but she couldn't help it. He was all consuming with his shit.

"I don't know. Look, I'll be back in town tomorrow. We can hook up and discuss everything. Are you and Zion attached at the damn hip?"

"Please stop cursing," Morgan grumbled with her narrowed eyes on Vadah.

Jordyn snorted as Vadah looked at Morgan.

"Jordyn, I'll call you when I get home," she said and ended the call. Vadah set her phone down and held a sleeping Ace tighter. "I'm not trying to replace your mom, Morgan. I would never do that."

Morgan shook her head.

"My auntie said you wanted my dad. He loves my momma," Morgan angrily said.

Vadah shook her head. She knew Tera wasn't fond of her, but to lie to a child about her was crossing the line.

"I don't, Morgan. I'm just here to watch you and your brother," Vadah assured her.

Morgan shrugged. The anger on her face slowly faded away.

"You promise?"

Vadah thought of Quan. He was everything she ever wanted in a man. Loving, sexy, and thoughtful. He was a good father, and he loved the Lord. He could be aggressive at times, but she even liked that side of him. What she didn't like was the pain she saw Morgan in. It made her sad, and if staying away from Quan would keep Morgan happy, then she would.

"I promise," Vadah said, and Morgan smiled.

Morgan jumped up from the bed and went to her side. She hugged Vadah's arm as Ace lightly snored on her.

"Good, because he only loves my momma," Morgan said, making Vadah swallow hard.

Thirty minutes later, they were ushered into the Amway Center. Vadah and the kids were shown to their seats along with two burly bodyguards. Vadah held a giddy Ace as the headphones rested over his ears. Cameras flashed as the players took the floor, making everyone in the arena go crazy.

"My daddy!" Morgan yelled and jumped up.

Quan winked at her before jogging over. He quickly hugged Morgan before ruffling Ace's hair. His amber hued eyes then gazed down at Vadah, and he made her gasp when he leaned down and kissed her cheek.

As Quan jogged back over to his teammates, Morgan stared at Vadah intently.

"He does that to my mommy too," she said and turned her attention back to Quan.

Vadah nodded. She believed that he could also do that to Tamm. What she wanted to know, however, was why at that exact moment had he done that to her?

"How you like the game?"

They were 35,000 feet in the air, and Vadah was beat. Ace, like always, rested on top of her as he snored lightly. Morgan sat in her seat behind them as well, lost in her dreams. Quan sat beside Vadah stretched out. His hand rested on her leg, and while she wanted to ignore it, she couldn't.

Everything with them felt so domesticated.

"Jordyn told me that you are cousins with Zion," she said, pushing his hand away.

Quan's eyes peered over at her curiously as he placed his hand back onto her thigh.

"Yeah, that's my first cousin on my pops' side. We more like brothers, though. Me, him, Zeke, and our cousin, Jigga. How did you like the game?" he asked again.

Vadah rubbed Ace's back, and he smiled in his sleep.

Quan chuckled as he stared at him.

"His lil chunky ass loves you. He was trying to walk earlier."

Vadah smiled at the thought of Ace walking.

"Yes, and he almost had it! He saw some candy in my bag on the floor and chose to crawl over to it instead of walking," she replied, making both of them laugh. "But to answer your question, you did okay. You was sleeping on Pierce when I told you to look out for him," she replied.

Quan sighed. His hand tightened on her leg as he looked straight ahead.

"Yeah, I underestimated that nigga. He was playing like it was the playoffs and shit. How Ace and Morgan do at the game?"

Vadah's cell vibrated, and she glanced down at her screen. She adjusted Ace so she could see the screen better, and the text slid across the long device.

Jase: Seen you on the TV. You fucking with that nigga Quan now? Hit me up, I miss your pretty ass.

"Who the fuck is that? Quan asked looking at the phone.

Vadah put her phone away and peered over at Quan. His thick brows were knitted together as he frowned at her. He was back in his suit and looking sexy as ever.

"This guy I thought could be something good but turned out to be something very bad," she replied, thinking back on her attractive ex-boyfriend.

"What was you in school for?"

"I haven't picked a major yet. Originally, it was for nursing, then I changed it to liberal arts. I honestly don't know what I want to do," she replied.

Quan pulled on his chin hairs as he stared straight ahead.

"Then why was you in school?"

Vadah shrugged.

"It felt like the right thing to do. Plus, I wanted to make my mom proud. She's very independent and has always been that way. She owns her own caregiving business. My father left when I was younger, and she went back to school to take care of us. I want to make her proud. Hell, that's the only reason why I took this job. She was ashamed of the way I looked in those bullshit ass videos, as you liked to call them."

Quan shook his head.

"I think me and my people are lucky. We always knew what we wanted to be in life. One of my cousins was big in the streets, but thankfully, he was lucky enough to walk away from that shit. I know for me, ball was always life. Before my pops died, he played that shit with me religiously. My mom saw that I liked it, and she put me in camps for it. Shit, they worked hard for my black ass to be able to do this shit, and that's why I spoil her ass rotten right now. I know you love your mom, but you can't live your life for her. Do what makes you happy, Vadah," he replied.

Vadah peered over at him and smiled.

"Even if that's doing videos?" she playfully asked.

Quan removed his hand and grabbed his son. He placed Ace inside the only room on the jet then came back to grab a sleeping Morgan. As he reclaimed his seat, he pulled a blunt from his pocket. Vadah watched him light it up as her eyes stayed glued to him.

"I'm sure that video shit was good money, but not all money is worth having. When you put your body on display like that, it brings different shit into your life. Bad vibes that you don't need, ma, and no real man is gone be cool with that. I know I wouldn't be," he expressed and hit the blunt.

Vadah shrugged. She understood where he was coming from but also hated feeling like someone was telling her what to do.

"I get that, but I'm grown. It was a legit way to make money, and I wasn't on the pole to get it."

Quan's eyes peered over at her as weed slipped from between his thick lips.

"You still made niggas' dicks hard, so does it matter if a pole was there or not? You should use this time while you working for me to think about your life and what you wanna do with it. You mad at what I said?" he asked.

Vadah shook her head. She frowned as she looked at everything except Quan. His words seemed like they were coming from a good place, but still, she took offense to them.

"I'm good, and instead of trying to father me, do that to

your kids. Morgan really needs you right now," she told him and pulled out her ear plugs.

She watched Quan shake his head before she tuned him out. As he smoked on his blunt, she listened to one of Jordyn's many playlists that she'd shared with her. Quan was cool but being so close to him and wrapped up in his world was maddening at times, and Vadah needed a break.

CHAPTER
Nine

"THAT WEED GOT YOU BUGGING. Come here."

Jordyn shook her head, and Zion laughed. They were on the beach in Miami in the middle of the night. Zion had hooked up with his cousins who had some legit ass weed, and they were next level high. Jordyn, who was high out of her mind, stood in her black one-piece swimsuit with the stomach cut out, frowning at Zion.

"I'm floating. Why the fuck am I floating?" she asked worriedly with her eyes widened.

Zion, clad in Burberry trunks and his diamond chain, laughed so hard his eyes watered. Jordyn was standing on the shore instead of the water, and the scene before him had him amused.

"Ma, nothing but reggie's for you from now on. You not floating. Come here, beautiful," he gently coaxed her.

Jordyn shook her head, refusing to move. Zion walked over to her and pulled her into his arms. His hands went down to her ample ass, and he squeezed it. He'd made sure she wore a cover-up earlier because the niggas in Miami had been staring at Jordyn like they'd never seen an ass before, but now that it was only them two on the beach, he was cool with her exposing her bottom.

"You okay? You scaring me, J."

Jordyn shook her head. The weed was too strong for her liking. That shit had her literally stuck.

"I'm high," she finally admitted, and Zion chuckled.

"I know. Guess what?"

Jordyn peered up at him, smiling.

"What?"

Zion groped her ass.

"You also beautiful as fuck. I've never seen anybody as beautiful as you," he admitted.

Jordyn gave him a silly grin, and he slapped her ass. Zion licked his lips as he found himself slapping that soft ass once more.

"Let's go back to the room," he said and picked Jordyn up.

It was Zion's birthday weekend, and he wanted to spend it with Jordyn. He'd been clear with his intentions with her, and in his words, he wanted all of her. Jordyn doted on the attention she was receiving from Zion and wouldn't have it any other way. He kept her in a bubble that she prayed didn't burst anytime soon.

Jordyn laughed as he carried her on the beach. She was the happiest she'd even been in her life.

"No, let's sleep here. Under the moon," she said and struggled to get down.

Zion chuckled as he helped her stand. They went back over to the large blanket he'd laid out for them, and Jordyn fell on her back. She stared up at the sky as Zion sat beside her. For several minutes, they allowed the ocean to be their soundtrack. The waves crashing on the shore had a calming effect on them.

"I wanna hit another blunt, but we so high, we might wander off into the ocean on some crazy shit," he said and shook his head.

Jordyn smiled, thinking another blunt was out of the question for her.

"Yes, I'm high as fuck. Tell me about your daughter," she insisted with her eyes on the sky.

Zion rubbed the back of his neck as he peered down at Jordyn.

"You stay trying to get me to talk. Tell me about your pops," he retorted.

Jordyn smiled lazily. Her fair skin was flushed, and her long hair was in its curly state all over her head, giving her an exotic island girl look.

"I already did, nigga. Talk."

Zion chuckled.

"You and that fucking mouth, man, but she's perfect. Her favorite color is pink."'

Jordyn laughed.

"Mine too, and sparkle," she mumbled.

Zion shook his head. His big hand fell on Jordyn's thigh as he thought of Zory.

"She loves cereal and pancakes. She hates eggs and chicken. Like, how the fuck she hate chicken? I still don't get that shit, but she do. She is scared of the dark but still wanna sleep with her lights off. She's crazy like that, but I love her. She's smart as fuck, and she loves to dance. She has dance class twice a week."

Jordyn placed her hand on top of his.

"I used to dance. Bezo's sister has a studio, and I went for years. Then my ass started getting so big that some of that shit was hard to do. I would have had to diet to stay doing ballet, so I let it go. My parents didn't trip, though. She sounds like an amazing little girl. I hope I get to meet her."

Zion leaned down and passionately kissed Jordyn on her lips. His eyes peered into hers as his tongue slid lovingly against hers.

"You will, sexy. Now get up and dance for me. I'ma put some music on," he said when he pulled back.

Jordyn smiled against his lips before kissing him again. She stood up, *still* high, and began to tootsie roll. Zion cracked up laughing as Pusha T's, "Circles" started to play on his phone.

Tell her throw that ass in a circle
Throw that ass in a circle
Tell her show what that work do
Tell her throw that ass in a circle
Tell her throw that ass in a circle, yeah

"I love Pusha!" Jordyn said and spun around. Fluidly, she moved her ass in a circle for Zion.

He sat up and popped her on the ass before she started to slowly move it for him. Zion became hypnotized, and before he could help himself, he was pulling Jordyn down onto his lap. His hands went between her soft thighs as he caressed her thick mound.

Jordyn gyrated on his lap as the music continued to play.

"Rub it," she whispered, wanting to get a release. One that wasn't initiated by her own fingers.

Zion pulled his bottom lip into his mouth. He pushed the thin fabric of her swimsuit to the side, and his fingers began to massage Jordyn's silky folds. She was velvety soft, and never in his twenty-one years of living had he been so excited to finger someone.

"I like you," he confessed as if she didn't know it.

Jordyn's head fell back on his shoulder. She closed her eyes as the wind kissed her skin.

"I like you too, and I don't usually like men."

Zion slowly rubbed at her pearl. The round and round motion nearly sent Jordyn over the edge.

"What's so different about me?" he asked and slowly inserted two of his fingers inside of her.

Jordyn whimpered.

"I feel spiritually in tune with you. It's past the physical, you know? You get me, and you see me. So many people don't really know what I am beyond my looks, or they just don't care to. You do," she whispered.

Zion curved his fingers inside of Jordyn and pressed down hard. His fingers moved at a rapid pace as he made her fall apart in his arms. Once he knew she was good, he pulled his fingers out of her and licked them clean before picking Jordyn up and carrying her back to the room.

The next day, Zion handled business while Jordyn looked at her grades online. They had dropped, and she knew her mom would soon be calling her. She shut her laptop and looked out at the water. They were at the Mandarin Oriental hotel, and Jordyn was in love with it. It was hands down one of the nicest suites she'd ever been in, and that was saying a lot since her parents spared no expenses when it came to raising her and her siblings.

Jordyn decided to check out her real dad's Facebook page and saw that he was out of town as well with his wife. She smiled as she stared at the photos of them doing tourist things in New York. Her thoughts ran wild as she imagined herself doing things like that with him.

Jordyn realized that something like traveling with Rome may never happen, and once again, her mood was killed. She shut her laptop and decided to take a quick shower. After she was cleaned and dressed in black a Kloset Envy midi dress with gold heeled Giuseppe's and wild, curly hair, she found Zion.

He was on the balcony finishing off a blunt while staring at the water. Jordyn walked up behind him and hugged his back. She'd never even thought of being with a man exclusively, but Zion was different. He made her think about things like relationships.

"You smell good as fuck," Zion said, inhaling her sweet scent.

The Tory Burch perfume was for sure placing him in a trance.

"Thank you. Are you ready?"

Zion nodded. He'd gotten dressed earlier and immediately started to check on his businesses while Jordyn rested. He was good and ready to fuck up some food.

"Yeah, let's go," he replied and tossed his blunt over the balcony.

Zion and Jordyn ate lunch at a small Cuban restaurant before Jordyn pulled him into a tattoo shop off N. Miami Ave. Zion, buzzing off the liquor, held Jordyn's hand tightly as she mulled over what to get.

"I don't know. I want something, but it has to be bomb. Like, I don't want a bunch of random fucking tattoos on me. All my tattoos mean something to me. Maybe we should go," Jordyn said.

Zion nodded. Shit, whatever she wanted to do was cool by him.

"What's that?" Jordyn asked, noticing a symbol in the book that she'd never seen before.

The tattoo artist who was struggling with not ogling Jordyn looked down at the paper.

"That's the new beginning tattoo," he replied.

Jordyn admired the beautiful symbol. She smiled as she leaned on Zion.

"I like that. Can I get that one on my ankle?"

The tattoo artist nodded. He eyed her shapely legs and swallowed hard. When he looked up, Zion was glaring at him.

"Nigga be easy," Zion warned, and the tattoo artist chuckled.

"It's all good, man. Let me get my gloves," he said and briskly walked away.

Jordyn laughed and pressed herself against Zion. She was having the time of her life and wasn't ready for the moment to end.

"You should get the tattoo. I know life is crazy for us, but we could be each other's new beginnings," she told him.

Zion swallowed hard. He was donned in all white. It was hot as fuck in Miami, and the clean linen he wore gave him some heat relief. He looked handsome in his attire, and Jordyn had been staring at him all day along with every other woman they passed. His fade was clean, and even his beard had been manicured. He was tap dancing on being pretty, but she would never tell him that.

Those hooded eyes of his with their syrupy brown color peered down at her, and he smiled.

"Maybe next time, beautiful," he said.

Jordyn was crushed but didn't let it show. She broke their gaze, and he kissed the top of her forehead, sensing she was hurt.

"You look so beautiful tonight," he whispered in her hair as the tattoo artist walked back over to them.

Jordyn rolled her eyes, hating how right it felt to be in his arms.

So beautiful, yet you couldn't commit to a little ass tattoo? Yeah, beautiful my ass.

Jordyn was snatched away from her thoughts when the gun pressed against her skin. She winced at how it hurt because she didn't love that kind of pain and closed her eyes until it was done.

After Jordyn was tatted up, the duo grabbed some more liquor and headed back to the room. Jordyn wanted to hit up Liv, but Zion felt like it was time to retire. Jordyn had been giving him the cold shoulder after he shot down her request for a tattoo, and he wanted to make it up to her.

Orally.

"Come here," he said, pulling her gently into the room.

Jordyn looked up at him as he pulled her into his arms, and she smiled.

"What?"

Zion shook his head. All day, he'd stolen glances at her. Soaking in her beauty.

"I wanna tell you some real shit, and I don't want you to get offended."

Jordyn nodded with a soft sigh, not sure what the fuck he was about to say.

"Just say it. I mean, you're not like Batman or anything, are you?"

Jordyn's question was so outlandish that it made Zion laugh hard as hell. He took her over to the soft, big bed, and they sat down.

"You wild as fuck for that one. Nah, I'm not Batman, man. When Zory's mom broke shit off with me, I was hurt. She was the only woman I ever loved. I turned into one of them bitter niggas, and I started hating women," he said, and Jordyn broke his gaze.

Zion pulled her onto his lap, making her dress rise above her ass. His hands gripped her cheeks as he looked her in the eyes.

"I don't know what the fuck this is, ma. I've never had no shit like this happen to me. Even with my ex, it was over time. It wasn't instant. I don't really believe in all that love at first sight shit, but I like the way you make me feel," he expressed to her.

Jordyn stared into his eyes with her heart pounding in her chest.

"And I like the way you make me feel."

Zion smirked at her.

"Can I really make you feel good?" he asked.

Jordyn dropped her head. Her high cheekbones darkened at his request. She shrugged, not sure if she was ready to go all the way, and Zion kissed her cheek. He stuck his face into the crook of her neck and slowly licked her soft skin.

"Let me taste you. I want you to cum in my mouth," he confessed in a husky tone.

Jordyn's sex clenched together at the sound of his dirty words.

"Okay," she quietly responded, and he laughed.

Zion placed Jordyn on the bed and took her clothes off. He turned on Maxwell because he knew how much she loved him, and as "This Woman" began to play, he feasted on her.

Jordyn's eyes took up permanent residence in the back of her head as Zion licked, sucked, and slurped on her pussy.

Her juices coated Zion's tongue in a way that made his dick immediately hard. He groaned deep in the back of his throat as he sucked on her clitoris. His fingers worked at Jordyn's snug tunnel, and within minutes, Jordyn was crying out at the top of her lungs.

CHAPTER

Ten

"ARE you willing to meet up with me?"

Just the sound of his voice angered Vadah. She groaned as she grabbed her glass. Her eyes skated around the inside of the bar, and she sighed. Like always, her ex-boyfriend was running late. Nigga couldn't be on time for shit.

"I don't know. I'm sure my mom told you about my job. It's very demanding. I was surprised I took today off," she replied as Quan's call clicked in, interrupting her current call.

Vadah sent his call to voicemail and looked around the room again for Jase.

"Yes, she did, and I don't know how to feel about that as well. You're so young. You should be focusing on school. Not babysitting some little kids of an NBA player. I can give you money if that's what you need," he replied.

Vadah shook her head as her brows furrowed. He had some nerve.

"Now, you can give me money? I don't need your child support now, *dad.* If I can get another off day, I might call you. Goodbye," she replied and ended the call.

"I see you still ice cold with your shit," Jase said as he walked up.

Vadah turned to him and smiled. Her anger with Quan and his controlling ways had pushed her into defense mode. Jase wasn't shit. He knew it and she did too, but she needed a release. Quan had her worked up, and Jase's long member would reap the benefits of that.

"Hey stranger," she said and stood.

Jase pulled Vadah into a hug and rubbed her ass. His tatted arms held her tightly as he embraced her.

"I'm glad to see you was thinking about a nigga."

Vadah rolled her eyes.

"Yes, I guess I was," she said, pulling back from the hug.

Vadah reclaimed her seat, and Quan called her again. Her eyes narrowed as she peered down at her screen.

"I need to take this," she said and quickly answered the call.

Quan breathed into the phone as the call connected.

"Come home," he demanded lowly.

Vadah pulled the phone away from her ear and looked at the name on the screen to make sure she wasn't bugging. Jase watched her carefully while ordering a drink.

"Is everything okay with the kids? Is it Tamm?"

"Just get here now," he grumbled and ended the call.

Vadah set her phone down, and Jase smirked at her. Time had been good to him. He wore black jeans with a black polo and multicolored Balenciaga sneakers. His fade was evenly cut, and his handsome, tawny brown face still made her insides churn with lust. Vadah licked her lips as Quan called her once more. She was beginning to worry as she abruptly stood up.

"That was my job. I need to go. I'm so sorry," she said and pulled out her keys.

Jase's thick brows dipped in confusion. He stood from his stool and pulled Vadah into his arms. Hugging her tightly, he kissed her forehead.

"When you get a minute, call me. I never got a chance to

apologize for all the shit I did to you. I was wrong, and I wanna show you a different side of me. Don't forget about a nigga, girl," he whispered before letting her go.

Jase's words made Vadah stare up at him. He shot her a playful smirk before sitting back down. She nodded and rushed off. Vadah exited the bar and jumped into her car. Her thoughts ran wild as she imagined Tamm being sicker or the kids needing assistance.

She rushed from downtown Detroit to West Bloomfield in record time, and as she pulled through the gates, Quan stood in the driveway smoking on a blunt. A look of worry sat on his handsome mug as he wore his navy pajama bottoms with no shirt and YSL slides. His amber hued eyes shot her way as she parked behind Tamm's Audi.

"Lord, please let Tamm be okay," she prayed before exiting her car.

"What's wrong?"

Quan stopped smoking on his blunt to walk over to Vadah. He tossed his blunt to the ground as he advanced on her.

"Morgan said you was on a date. What the fuck is she talking about?"

"What?"

Vadah was shocked and confused. She laughed nervously, and Quan grabbed the back of her neck. As he leaned down, his warm breath fanned her face. He sniffed her blouse before looking into her eyes.

"Was you really on a date?"

Vadah tried to pull back, and Quan tightened his grip. It wasn't enough to scare her, but it did piss her off.

"*Quan*, let me go. I am not Tamm," she said through gritted teeth.

Quan snarled. Vadah slightly shoved his chest, and he passionately attacked her with his thick lips. Vadah gasped as he kissed her like she'd never been kissed before.

"Quan, *no*," she whined as he sucked on her bottom lip.

His kisses tasted like heaven. Vadah's body immediately caved into him as he kissed her breath away. He picked her up and carried her around the mini mansion. Quan never broke the kiss as he took Vadah to the guesthouse. Vadah pulled back from his soft lips as he opened the door. Her chest heaved up and down as she peered into his eyes.

"Stop, we can't. This is wrong, and I promised Morgan I would stay away from you."

Quan's brows dipped. He kissed her again and took her into the home. As Quan locked the doors, Vadah watched him intently.

"Was you on a date?" he asked again as he took her into the bedroom.

Quan dropped Vadah onto the bed and stepped out of his slides. Vadah lay motionless on the pillow top mattress as she watched him slide down his pajama pants.

Yes, she'd thought of him many nights, but to have him in front of her bed de-clothing was unreal. His body was ripped thanks to his healthy eating and regular workouts. He had just enough tattoos to turn her on, and he was hung. His member, not even at full erection, stuck out of his electric blue boxers, ready to do some damage as he licked his lips.

The glare in his eyes wasn't lost on Vadah as she held her chest. She was frightened and wet at the same time.

"Quan, you need to leave. Please get your shit and go. I didn't sign up for this."

Quan nodded. He took off his boxers and Vadah's PC muscles clenched together at the sight of his dick. It was pretty, perfectly colored, and thick. Just the right length, and as Quan stroked it slowly back and forth, Vadah's sex grew wetter.

"Fuck all that. I need you to answer my fucking question," Quan retorted and grabbed her ankle. Vadah's breathing grew ragged as he pulled off her slides. Next came her jeans, and her tongue grew heavy. Quan shook his head as he looked over her bare sex. "Where the fuck your underwear at?"

Vadah cleared her throat. Quan was scaring the shit out of her while turning her on at the same damn time.

"I planned to have sex," she nervously admitted.

Quan's head snapped back as if he was insulted. He leaned down and grabbed the bottom of Vadah's chin. Her chest heaved up and down as she stared into his eyes.

"I'm sorry," she squeaked, not sure what to say.

Quan glared at her while piercing her with his amber eyes.

"Take that shirt off and get on your knees. If I hear 'bout you trying to fuck another nigga, it's gone' be a fucking problem. Now, turn around," he demanded and let her chin go.

Vadah moved swiftly to do as he'd told her to do. She pulled off her Allure Boutique chiffon top, and Quan swallowed hard at the sight of her perky, full breasts. Vadah flipped onto all fours and dipped her back. Out the corner of her eye, she watched Quan slip on a condom before he grabbed her hip. His soft, thick lips pressed against the top of her shoulder as he held his dick at her opening.

"I can't stop thinking about you. I even feel fucked up because this shit is so close to home, but I'm not with Tamm. I haven't been with her for a while now. I see good shit happening for us, Vadah. Don't go looking for dick from no other niggas. Okay?" he asked and rubbed the head at her sopping wet center.

Vadah exhaled. Her body shuddered as she shook her head.

"I can't hurt Tamm," she murmured softly.

Quan kissed the back of her neck and slowly pushed himself inside of her. The thick intrusion caused her to whimper out in pleasure. His tongue slid into her ear, and he licked it sensually before pulling back.

"I'ma take care of everything. Do you trust me?"

Vadah nodded with her eyes closed.

"I do," she whispered in a breathy tone.

Quan slid deeper into her and kissed her neck again.

"Then don't worry about shit. I got you, now open this pussy up for me," he replied and pulled back so that he could pound into her sex.

"When are you coming home?" Vadah asked as she dried off Ace.

He laughed and fell onto the bed. She smiled as his short, stubby legs slowly raised. While giggling his head off, he took one shaky step before falling back onto the comforter.

"Soon, what's wrong?" Jordyn asked.

Vadah groaned. She was happy her girl was falling in love, but damn, she needed her too.

"It's just a lot. I had sex with Quan…. a few times," she whispered.

"What! When? Bitch, you been holding out on me," Jordyn based.

Vadah's shoulders fell. She glanced up, and Tamm's sister stood in front of her with a scowl on her pretty, caramel toned face. Vadah took a deep breath and sighed.

"Can I help you?" she asked as Ace pulled on her arm until he was able to stand.

Teresa looked around the room in the guest house and shook her head. Vadah watched Teresa's eyes zeroed in on a pair of Quan's shoes that sat near the side of the bed, and she scoffed.

"I fucking knew it! I've been watching them cameras and waiting on y'all to slip up. Bitch, you gotta go!" Teresa yelled and slapped Vadah so hard she dropped the phone.

Teresa didn't give Vadah time to recover as she commenced to punching her in the face. Vadah, not wanting to hurt Ace, took the licks until the maid walked by the room. The maid stopped cleaning to break up the fight, and Vadah picked up a crying Ace, who she'd fallen on top of. He hugged her tightly as Teresa fought with the maid.

"Bitch give me my nephew!" she yelled and snatched Ace out of Vadah's arms.

Vadah stood slowly as she felt blood drip from her nose.

"Get your shit and go. I won't fucking say it again," Teresa angrily raged.

Ace cried as he reached out for Vadah. Looking at his chunky, sad face, Vadah's eyes watered. She wanted to beat the shit out of Teresa as she stood before her.

"Do I need to set him down?" Teresa asked and took a step toward Vadah.

Vadah looked at her lil Ace one last time before walking over to the closet. She could have put up a fight, but for him and Morgan, she would let it be. Now, if she was to see Teresa on the streets, it would be another story, but while in the house, she wouldn't fight her again.

Quietly, Vadah packed up her things. As she grabbed her purse, Teresa smiled, showing off her huge dimples.

"And leave all the fucking keys. My sister is sick, and you fucking her baby daddy. It's a special place in hell for hoes like you," she spat.

Vadah nodded. She knew the truth, and so did Teresa.

"I want you to keep this same energy if you see me on the street, Teresa. Please do that," Vadah said pulling the keys off her key ring.

Teresa laughed as she ignored Ace's cries.

"Bitch, ain't nobody worried about your broke, slutty ass. Bitch had to be a babysitter just to pay the bills. I guess the rappers got tired of fucking your trick ass," she muttered vehemently.

Vadah smiled. She grabbed her purse and the handle to her rolling cart. She looked at Ace, and her heart ached. She would miss him and Morgan terribly.

"If you were this invested into your own marriage, maybe you could have kept your nigga happy. Bye, Ace, I love you," Vadah said before walking off.

"Well, he don't love you! And neither do Morgan!" Teresa yelled to Vadah's retreating back.

Vadah held her tears in until she was in her car. As she pulled away from Tamm's home Quan began to call her. Vadah wanted to answer, tell on Teresa, and return to the place that she'd grown to love, but she didn't. She had been fucking Tamm's ex in the guest house, and even though it felt good, she knew the shit was wrong. Quan's situation was too much for her, and it was best for her to walk away instead.

Vadah went to the closest gas station and pulled up to a pump so she could call him back.

"Hey, I just talked to Teresa. I had to tell that ugly bitch off. What the fuck we do is none of her business. Did she really jump on you?" he angrily asked.

Vadah wiped her face. She was so sad that it was hard for her to talk.

"SaQuan, I like you. When I saw you at the club, I was like 'damn, he's the shit.' From the way you love your kids to how good you take care of their mom, you are a good man. I just don't think you will ever be *my* man. I love your kids, and I'm going to miss them terribly, but I need to walk away. No matter what Tamm says, we shouldn't have been fucking in that guesthouse. It wasn't right, Quan. I can't do this anymore. So, this is where we say goodbye. Please tell Tamm how sorry I am," Vadah replied before ending the call.

She then powered off her phone and headed to a place she hadn't been to in months.

Home.

CHAPTER
Eleven

"CLOSE YOUR EYES," he said, and Jordyn giggled.

She was so nervous that she would have peed herself if she hadn't relieved her bladder already. In the distance, she could hear the water. It even misted against her skin as he took her deeper into the cave.

"Can I look now?"

Zion nodded.

"Yeah, open those beautiful ass eyes up of yours, baby," he lovingly said.

Jordyn slowly opened her eyes and gasped. They called it the mermaid cave, and it was breathtakingly beautiful to Jordyn. Her eyes sparkled as she took in how gorgeous it was.

"Is this nice?" Zion asked, peering over at her.

Instead of going home, he'd decided to take Jordyn on yet another adventure. It was reckless to run from your problems, but damn it felt good to have an escape. To be away with someone who made shit bearable. Zion wasn't ready for the moment to end, so there he was with Jordyn in Hawaii, venturing into caves and shit. Like he didn't have a shit load of things waiting at home for him. Like he didn't have a daughter looking for his face.

It was selfish as fuck, and he knew that it would have to eventually end, but he wanted it to last for as long as it could.

Jordyn's head whipped his way. She wore an emerald green two-piece bathing suit that had all her goodies out. Zion had been threatening tourists and locals for openly admiring her. Jordyn was beautiful wherever she went, that much was clear.

"I love this, Zion. I've never seen anything so amazing," she whispered in awe.

Zion walked up behind her and pulled her into his arms.

"I know," he said, thinking of her.

Jordyn blushed as he kissed her soft neck.

"I saw you last night," she quietly told him.

Zion tried to let her go, and she placed her hands on top of his. She'd been asleep in the villa, but the sounds of a young girl laughing had jarred her from her sleep. She'd snuck up on Zion and caught him watching his daughter's performance in dance class. She looked so beautiful and was so well trained on the dance she was doing.

Jordyn noticed Zion's teary eyes, and she chose to not impose on his moment. Instead, she allowed him to have it.

"Your mother always FaceTime's you at her events?"

Zion nodded.

"Yeah, she does."

Jordyn nodded, trying to find a gentle way to say the things that were on her mind regarding Zion and his daughter.

"The only thing better than that would be for you to go there, right?"

Zion's teeth nipped at Jordyn's skin.

"Not now, J," he told her, not wanting to talk about it. He let Jordyn go and watched her go under the greenish blue water. She looked so happy, so full of life, and her happiness made him happy.

Back and forth, Jordyn swam, smiling until she finally

swam back over to him. Zion pulled her soaking wet body up on him, and she wrapped her legs around his waist. The island they were on was so peaceful that it really wasn't fair. Without the noise from the city, they were able to enjoy nature.

Jordyn had truly been at peace for the last five days that they'd been there.

"You need to go back to school?" he asked her.

Jordyn shook her head, ignoring the guilt she felt for doing so poorly in her studies.

"No, I don't. I told you I'm good. Let's go do some more exploring," she replied before kissing him passionately.

For hours, they hung out, living like nomads. Jordyn rode alongside Zion, and they toured the island. When the sun fell, they retreated to the villa, and Zion called his mom to check up on his daughter while Jordyn returned her mom's phone calls.

"What are you doing? You haven't called me in days, and I don't like that. I feel like you're hiding something," her mom insisted.

Jordyn pulled off her clothes and stepped into the large bathroom. She turned on the shower and looked at herself in the mirror.

"I'm not, I swear," she replied, noticing her obvious tan lines. She held a beautiful, sun kissed looked that she loved.

Her mom sighed into the phone, and she felt bad because she was hiding things that she knew her mom wouldn't approve of.

"I need you home with me. You're still my baby, Jordyn," her mom, Logan, told her.

Jordyn smiled. She loved her family so much.

"And you're still the best, finest momma in the world. Can I call you back? I have to number two," she said truthfully.

Logan laughed.

"You used to bust in the damn bathroom when I was in

there, and now you want privacy? Yeah, okay. I'll let you go. I love you, Jordyn Monet Flint."

Jordyn watched Zion step into the bathroom with a blunt, and she swallowed hard at the sight of him.

"I love you too, Mommy."

She set her phone down and rushed over to the toilet. She wasn't sure if it was the food or what, but her stomach was killing her. Zion cracked the window and sat on the edge of the tub.

Jordyn nervously glanced over at him, and he smiled.

"Baby, we okay. You can shit. Do you," he said, and she did.

Hell, she wouldn't have been able to wait any longer even if she wanted to.

"Yours don't even smell that bad," he said jokingly, and she covered her face.

Jordyn literally let a little loose and flushed the toilet every few seconds so that the bathroom wouldn't be unbearable for him.

"Zion, I don't need you to ever know what my shit smells like."

Zion passed her the blunt and kissed her lips. He sat back on the edge of the tub and admired her naked, raw beauty. She was so fucking gorgeous to him.

"Stop it. Play me something," he said, addicted to the nice ass soundtracks that Jordyn had saved on her phone.

Jordyn blew the weed smoke out of her mouth and grabbed her phone. She turned to 6lack, and Zion listened to the song.

I'm running low so don't play with my time
I'm searching, but it's nothing left to find
Send out a call, but no one's on the line
So if you want it, please make up your mind

Please make up your mind
I don't wanna lose myself loving you, loving you

Zion listened to the lyrics, and his eyes connected with Jordyn's. She passed him back the blunt and wiped herself off after flushing the toilet for the thousandth time.

"That shit good. Who that?" he asked as he put the blunt out.

Jordyn stood up, and his eyes went to the apex of her thighs.

"6lack," she replied and washed her hands.

Zion nodded, liking how the music sounded as he dropped his own swimming trunks. Jordyn's eyes fell to his half erect member, and she cleared her throat.

"It's pretty," she said, amazed by how smooth and long it was.

Zion chuckled. He grabbed his meaty dick and gently stroked it.

"Please don't call my shit pretty. Come on, pretty eyes, let's take a shower," he said and let his dick go.

Jordyn continued to stare at his long member until he pulled her into the large glass shower. Zion took her under the largest showerhead and pulled her in front of him. He grabbed some soap and began to rub it all over her body as the water washed away the dirt from their skin.

Jordyn closed her eyes and moaned at how good it felt.

"Stop moaning like that, J. You got my dick hard as fuck," Zion said and poked her with his erection.

Jordyn moaned again, and he spun her around. Zion picked Jordyn up, and like his penis had a mind of his own, it stuck up and started to rub against her slick opening.

Zion pulled Jordyn's bottom lip into his mouth as he slowly, very slowly, pushed his large head into her sex.

Jordyn moaned, loving the intrusion until he pushed into her so much that it hurt. She winced, and he pulled back.

"I'm sorry but come get it off. I need to nut, baby," he told her and pulled her out of the shower.

Jordyn smiled as he led her into the bedroom. Zion fell back onto the bed with his rock-hard erection, and Jordyn climbed onto his lap. She grabbed his penis with lustful eyes and started to stroke it up and down.

"Yeah. Like that, but get it wet, J," he said and closed his eyes.

Jordyn allowed saliva to trail from her mouth to his beautiful dick, and she stroked it. Up and down, her hand moved as she allowed his moans to guide her.

"Damn, ma. I can't wait to be up in you. I know it's good," Zion said, feeling his nut build up.

Jordyn leaned down and licked the head of his penis, liking the salty taste of his pre-cum. It wasn't nasty like women claimed that it was.

"It is, baby. This will be the best, wettest, tightest little pussy you ever had," she whispered to him, and Zion's breathing grew ragged as he shot off in her hand.

On their last day in Hawaii, Zion and Jordyn visited a sacred temple called Hikiau Heiau. It was a raised, slated lava rock that dated back to the 18th century. Jordyn being Jordyn had long ago read about it and was anxious to pray on it. She didn't attend church every Sunday, but she loved the Lord. She knew he who was and had even received the Holy Spirit when she was fifteen. It was, however, the religious church people that kept her away from a place that was supposed to be about God.

"You sure we good?" Zion nervously asked, not wanting the fucking lava to erupt.

Jordyn and their tour guide both smiled.

"Yes, we're good. Come on, let's pray, baby," she told him and pulled him over to the side of the rock.

They were both dressed in all white, and while Zion wore a white Supreme baseball cap, Jordyn had her hair in a long braid to the back. She dropped down to her knees, and Zion slowly followed suit. She grabbed his hand and started off the prayer.

"God, this wasn't necessary. I believe that you are with us at all times, but I do feel a strong connection to you here. Zion and myself… we need you. You brought us together, and now we need you to keep working on us. I need to fix my issues with Rome, and Zion… He needs peace, Lord. Please grant my baby peace in his heart, his mind, and his soul. I hear him when he sleeps. He's so troubled. So angry, and it scares me, God. I don't wanna lose him when I just got him. Help him be better for Zory, Lord. Please. In Jesus name, we pray. Amen,"

Zion's lone tear fell from his eye, and he briskly wiped it away.

"Amen," he said and pulled Jordyn into his arms. Zion hugged Jordyn tightly as his heart thundered in his chest. "Thank you," he whispered into her hair.

Partying with your girl and having fun was cool, but damn, to have someone pray for him was on another level. Zion realized at that moment that Jordyn's outward appearance was gorgeous as fuck, but inside of her was where her real beauty lied.

She was one of the best things to ever fucking happen to him. So good that his mind started to tell him that he would hurt her too, much like he was hurting Zory, because the truth was, he was still at war within himself. So, until he fixed his problems, he wouldn't be good for anyone.

"Hey, stranger! Where you been? You never called me back that one day!"

Vadah looked at Jordyn and shook her head. Instead of her usual, pretty appearance, Vadah looked tired. She wore faded leggings with an oversized tee and Fresh Prince of Bel-Air baseball cap. Jordyn pulled Vadah into a hug, and Vadah quickly pulled back.

"Just signing up for classes. I've been calling you for weeks now. I know you have Zion, but you do know its life outside of him, right?" Vadah asked.

Jordyn frowned at her girl. She was close to cursing her out until she noticed that Vadah had been crying. Jordyn grabbed Vadah's hand and led her to a table in the courtyard.

"Look, I'm sorry. Things with me and Zion are moving fast, but we're good together. He gets me, and he helps with my pain. You know how hurt I am behind my dad, Vadah. When I'm with Zion, none of that pain exists. It's hard to explain, but he's my medicine. I'm falling in love with him," Jordyn admitted.

Vadah nodded with pursed lips. She looked down at her phone before staring back up at Jordyn.

"I get it, but you can't rely on him to be happy, Jordyn. That's not realistic. I have to go, but you should take it easy.

Finish school and take your time with Zion. I'll talk to you later," Vadah said and left the table.

Jordyn frowned, shocked by her girl's words when her cell started to vibrate. She ignored two calls from her mom and was about to put her phone way when she noticed that Zion was blowing her up. She immediately took the call while grinning.

"Hey."

"What's up? You out of class?"

Jordyn smiled harder at the sound of his voice.

"Um yeah, you here?" she asked and looked around campus.

Zion sighed as he sat outside of his daughter's school watching her play at the school's playground with the other kids.

"Nah, I was thinking 'bout you. Can you meet up with me? I'm kind of fucked up right now," he admitted.

Jordyn rose to her feet and quickly gathered her things before heading for her car.

"Sure, I'm heading to your place now," she replied and ended the call.

It took Jordyn half an hour to get to Zion's home. His truck was already parked in the driveway, and his front door was unlocked. Zion sat in his living room with Sports Center on and a drink in his hand. An angry scowl sat on his handsome face as Jordyn entered the room.

She spotted him and immediately noticed his bruised-up face.

"What happened?"

Zion cleared his throat. He'd come dangerously close to touching the nigga responsible for his pain, but it didn't end well. Gunshots were fired, and he'd ended up wrecking his Impala. He was cool, just angry that he didn't succeed in killing him.

"If I was a killer, would you still wanna fuck with me?" he asked, making her frown.

Jordyn took a step back and cleared her throat. She'd been to his grow houses. Saw his degrees, and even witnessed him talking with his lawyers. He seemed as legit as one could be in that line of work. Jordyn was perturbed and didn't understand why he would call himself a killer.

"Zion, what the fuck are you talking about?"

Zion sat up and set his glass down. The fear in Jordyn's tone told him he needed to chill out.

"Nothing, I'm tripping. I got into a car accident. I didn't mean to scare you," he replied.

Jordyn stared at him with narrowed eyes.

"Zion, I know we watch a lot of hood movies. *Belly, Paid In Full*, you know, shit like that. Those movies are entertaining to look at, but I'm not about that life. I wasn't brought up in it, and I won't live in that life. I don't find that kind of shit exciting. Okay?" Zion nodded. "Now, I'm going to ask you this, and I want you to be honest. Are you in the streets?" she asked.

Zion immediately shook his head.

"Nah, I'm not," he claimed while gazing up at her.

Jordyn cleared her throat and went over to him. She sat down and tenderly touched all his bruises.

"Why don't you go see her? Please," she quietly said.

Zion shook his head. He pulled Jordyn into a hug and buried his face in her neck. Like always, she smelled so good to him.

"Not yet. Let's go lay down."

Jordyn wanted to say more. Instead, she nodded and went upstairs with Zion. They stripped down to their underwear and climbed into bed. Zion hugged Jordyn from the back as she watched old episodes of Sex and the City. Being in her presence gave him a peaceful feeling, and he enjoyed it. He wanted to spill his deep, dark secrets to her, but he didn't. He was worried it would push her away, so he kept them to himself.

"I just love her hair," Jordyn gushed, raving over Carrie Bradshaw's hair.

Zion looked at the TV screen and frowned.

"Your shit looks way better than that, ma," he told her, and she smiled.

Jordyn playfully rolled her eyes.

"You would say that."

Zion gently poked her with his semi-erection as he licked his lips.

"'Cause it's true. You're fucking beautiful, Jordyn. I can't tell you that shit enough, ma," he replied.

Jordyn's cheeks darkened.

"As well on the inside?" she quietly asked.

Zion lovingly kissed the back of her head.

"*Especially*, on the inside. The person who don't have you in their life is losing out," he replied, and immediately, his thoughts were once again on Zory.

Guilt washed over Zion, and he let go of Jordyn to fall back on the bed. Jordyn glanced back at him and smiled before finishing off her show. As she thought of how happy she was with him, Zion thought of Zory. His life, the shit he was doing, was catching up to him, and he was running out of ways to escape it.

Jordyn provided a beautiful distraction. She literally placed him in a bubble where none of the bullshit mattered, but even the bubble was starting to deflate. Zion was running out of ways to escape his demons and was waiting for it to all fall down.

Because he knew that eventually, it would.

CHAPTER
Twelve

TWO MONTHS LATER, Jordyn stood nervously on the doorsteps. It was ten in the morning. The fall weather was going from cool to cold; still, she was covered in a light sheen of sweat. Her thoughts were of her real father. No longer could she do the stalking and wondering. She needed more.

Jordyn rang the bell again, and minutes later, Rome's beautiful wife came to the door smiling. The moment she pulled it back, she knew who Jordyn was. Her mouth fell open as she stared Jordyn's way.

Jordyn studied the woman who her father had married. She looked nothing like her mother. Rome's wife was Chaldean with pale skin and a shapely figure. Her inky black hair was long and hung past the middle of her back. She had mahogany brown eyes with full lips and a heart-shaped face. To Jordyn, she could have easily passed for a Kardashian minus the surgery on the body.

"Please come in," Maniyla insisted.

Jordyn stepped in and glanced around. The two-story home was beautiful. It was on the smaller scale compared to the place her parents resided in, but still, it was lovely. The décor had earth tones with a lot of watercolor artwork.

Jordyn followed Maniyla into the living room and sat next to her on the cream leather sofa. Jordyn was so nervous; she wasn't sure what to say or do. Her eyes studied the photos that sat on the wall in the living room in beautiful, gold-plated frames. She saw that Rome's wife was holding a small baby in some of the photos, and her eyes widened.

"That's our son. He passed away from SIDS, and um… I went on to have a miscarriage a year after that, which turned into me hemorrhaging. I can't have any kids," Maniyla said and cleared her throat.

Jordyn swallowed hard.

"I'm sorry to hear that. He was beautiful."

Maniyla nodded while still looking Jordyn's way.

"It's still fresh, so it's hard to discuss him, but let's talk about you. Your father is so proud of you."

Jordyn's brows pinched together.

"He is?"

Maniyla placed her hands on her lap.

"Yes, he is! He always talks about you, and we follow you. It's hard for him, though, Jordyn. He doesn't necessarily get along with your mother and her husband. When you were younger, an altercation happened between the two, and things got heated. Your father has a lot of issues with Logan."

Jordyn scooted away from Maniyla and stared down at her nails for a moment. She had gone all out to see Rome. She'd gotten her hair curled at the beauty shop. Her nails and toenails were painted a natural pink while she wore dark pants with a black blouse and black Christian Louboutin pumps. She thought she looked pretty. She wanted him to see her. Be in awe of the beauty that she'd blossomed into, all without his help.

What Jordyn didn't sign up for was a walk down memory lane with a bitch she didn't even know.

"Is Rome here?" Jordyn asked.

Maniyla swallowed hard.

"Actually, no, your *father* isn't here. I can take your number down, and the moment he comes back, I'll call you. This has been a long-time coming, sweetie," she replied.

Jordyn took a deep breath and exhaled. She was doing everything in her power to remain calm.

"Okay, that'll work," Jordyn replied, anxiously waiting for the moment he would call.

"Aye, man, you know she was on that shit with that nigga? He set up some people, and the shit backfired. You know how the game go!" the man angrily yelled.

Zion shook his head. He paced the floor in front of the man with anger surging through him like hot lava.

"You excusing a mother being taken away from her child, muthafucka? Is that what the fuck you doing?"

The young man with blood dripping down his face vehemently shook his head.

"Nah… nah, I'm just saying. She was on that coke and shit. She was getting strung out, nigga," he nervously said.

Zion stopped pacing and closed his eyes as he thought of his deceased ex. How lost he noticed she was becoming, yet he ignored it. She didn't wanna be with him anymore, and he was bitter behind it. Selfishly, he ignored the signs that were right before his eyes. She was on coke. Involved with a man who had put her on that shit, and now she was dead behind it.

"Nigga, nothing excuses that shit. Tell me where he's at."

The victim groaned. The cold post he was chained to was making his arms go numb.

"Come on, man. I ain't even seen your face! I won't say shit. Man, I got a daughter to take care of," he pleaded.

Zory. She constantly ran through Zion's mind. He groaned, wishing he had it in him to kill the man before him. He pulled out his cellphone and saw a text from Jordyn that made his heart race.

Your bitch ass brother is up here harassing me.

Zion put his phone away, and with one swift motion, he punched the man with so much force that he knocked him out. He then unchained him and left the raggedy, abandoned home. He jumped in his car and drove to Jordyn's photo shoot that she was doing with his photographer for his website.

The shoot was located on Detroit's east side, and it took Zion forty minutes to get there. He parked next to Zeke's Mercedes Wagon then took off his gloves and his black hoodie before exiting his vehicle.

Jordyn's angry voice could be heard from the hallway as he approached the studio.

"But you have a fiancée, right? I'm curious as to why the fuck you feel the need to run behind me, especially since I'ma hoe," Jordyn said with anger in her light tone.

Zeke stood not too far from her with a snarl marring his handsome face.

"Ma, you's definitely a hoe. A pretty one, but a hoe, nonetheless. Bed hopping on brothers and shit is not a good look. Shit, I wanna hit it. You caused all types of drama in my life with yo slick ass comment to Dream. You need to pay me back with that pussy."

A few men laughed while Jordyn rushed to get dressed. She slipped on her shoes, forcing herself to remain calm. All it would take was one phone call for Zeke to be on the news. Her family did not play about her.

"Damn, it's like that, nigga? You on this simp ass shit?" Zion asked with his deep voice garnering all the attention in the room.

Zeke turned to him. He smiled and waved his head.

"Simp? Shit, I'm just making sure these hoes know they place. I see you the one out here trying to save them," he jested.

Zion nodded. The days' worth of stress came crashing down on him, and he took it out on Zeke. With more force than he'd given the nigga from the abandoned home, Zion beat Zeke's ass.

Zeke took the beating Zion blessed him with as people struggled to break them apart.

"What the hell is going on?" Zion's mother yelled as she ran into the room.

Zion stopped fighting his brother at the sound of his mother's voice, and Jordyn swallowed hard. Everything had gotten way out of control, and a part of her felt guilty about it.

"Nigga, you need to leave," Zion angrily told Zeke.

Zeke breathed hard while blood seeped from his lip and the cut on top of his chin.

"Ma, your son is fighting me over somebody I was with first. He wanna fight for her when he won't even chase his own daughter. What kind of shit is that?"

Zeke's words made a few people gasp. Everyone knew Zory was off limits. Zion pulled out his gun, and his mom's heart dropped. Her son was more lost than she ever imagined. Jordyn, not thinking, and only reacting, walked over to Zion and grabbed his face. He hadn't pointed his weapon, but the cold look in his eyes scared her. She didn't want him to do something that he couldn't take back.

"Please relax. Stop. Stop, Zion," she whispered.

Zion stared down into her eyes with rage in his heart. He was tired. *So,* fucking tired of life.

"I fucked up," he confessed in a throaty tone.

His mother made all the staff leave before locking the door. Zion gazed down at Jordyn, and he cleared his throat.

"I was mad at her. She just stopped loving me one day, and that shit hurt. I cut her off, and when she started coming around looking crazy, I ignored it. I was so mad at her that I told myself that I didn't care. That she deserved it and shit. I not only put my daughter at risk, but I also helped her moms get killed. Maybe if I would have said something, even took Zory, she would have left him. Maybe..."

Jordyn shook her head. Behind her, Zion's mother silently wept while his brother dropped his head. Their beef was now no more. He was more concerned with his brother's wellbeing.

"It was her fate. You didn't kill her, and you can't chase down the people who did without them possibly killing you in the process. She doesn't need to lose two parents, Zion. That wouldn't be fair to her," Jordyn told him.

Zion stared into her eyes with wet lenses.

"I feel so fucking guilty. I can't face her. Not after I watched her mom self-destruct like that. I can't do that shit," he replied.

Zion's eyes filled to the brim with tears, yet he refused to let them fall. He put his gun away, and his mother pulled him into a tight embrace. Jordyn stepped back, and Zeke walked over to her. Half of his face was already swelling from his beat down.

"I'm sorry," he grunted before going over to Zion. He joined in on the hug, and Jordyn quietly exited the room.

The next few days were a blur to Zion. He temporarily shut down his shops and sought counseling to help with him losing his daughter's mother.

What he thought would be a quick process turned into months, and before he realized it, he'd gone close to a year without speaking to or seeing Jordyn. Eight months without her voice or seeing her pretty face. Eight months without her witty comebacks or soulful playlist. However, the bond that he was reestablishing with his daughter was his number one priority, so he told himself that when the time was right, he would reach out to her.

When the right time came, he would try his best to bring her back into his life.

CHAPTER
Thirteen

"IT'S my hope that **Vadah's Haven** can be a place for the innocent youth to find refuge. With this money, I will do just that. I already have a small building and I'm working on getting more grants. I am incredibly grateful to give back," Vadah said and smiled at the room of two hundred.

Her parents stood front and center, clapping harder than anyone else. Vadah's eyes connected with the one person she couldn't live without, and she sighed in contentment. Life was finally turning around for her. She'd found her passion, which was caregiving like her mother, and was now a business owner. She was still in school and looking to open her first business in a few short weeks.

Vadah's Haven would be a government funded center that provided recreational activities for children with low income. It would be like a Boys and Girls Club while also offering daycare services. Vadah was anxious to get it open. She was also extremely tired, considering she had a lot on her plate.

Adir rested peacefully in Jase's arms as she looked at them.

"Real quick, before you go," the professor said, stopping Vadah.

Vadah smiled although she wanted to roll her eyes. She'd been up since six that morning and was yearning for her bed.

"Yes," she politely replied.

The professor smiled at her as he tucked his hands into his pants.

"We're so proud of you and all that you've done. Your grades are the best they've ever been, and we know this is just the beginning with you. There is a school luncheon tomorrow that we want you to attend. Some heavy hitters will be there, and you could possibly find more sponsors for your building. Okay?"

Vadah nodded, loving the sound of that.

"Okay," she replied, and the professor grinned at her before walking away.

Vadah rushed over to her baby and grabbed him as Jase looked her over.

"You did good. We proud of you," he declared.

"We are," her father joined in.

Vadah nodded. She looked at Jase and her father then sighed. Life without Quan, and his kids had been bleak for her. She'd found out she was pregnant a month after leaving the guesthouse and was determined to make something of herself for her child. She signed back up for school and used all the money she had for investments. Vadah was now financially stable, and more importantly, she was happy.

Forgiving her father wasn't easy, but she'd let him back into her life along with Jase. Jase wasn't Quan, but he did make her smile, and she believed in her heart that he had changed.

"Thank you, guys. I really wanna skip dinner and go home. I'm beat," she admitted and laughed.

Her mom smiled as she rubbed her arm.

"I know you are. Can I take him home with me? You look like you could use the break."

Vadah stared down at her sleeping son. God, he was Ace's twin. He looked so much like him that it was crazy.

"I don't know," she mumbled, not wanting to let her baby go.

Vadah's father, James, grabbed her son and smiled at her lovingly.

"You need the rest, sweetie. Even Superwoman gets a break," he said and passed the baby to Vadah's mom.

Vadah exhaled, and Jase pulled her to his side.

"Come on, I'll take you home," he said, making Vadah bite her bottom lip.

Vadah gave her mom Adir's diaper bag before leaving the room. She left the college with Jase, and he took her back to her condo that she'd upgraded. She now lived in a two-bedroom, two-bathroom space. It was bigger and was the best fit for her and Adir.

As Vadah walked into her place, Jase rushed to the living room. He turned on the TV, and basketball fell onto the screen. Vadah's heart stopped beating as she watched Quan run up and down the court like a madman. It was an old game that was on a sports show. The show's host discussed Quan and how savagely he played as Vadah stared at her TV.

"When you gone' tell him?"

"Huh?"

Jase frowned. His brows furrowed, and he shook his head.

"For months, you done told me you would let that nigga know about his son. This shit is not cool, Vadah," Jase expressed.

Vadah walked off and headed for her bedroom. She sat at the edge of her bed as Jase trudged into the room. She looked him over, admiring his outfit for the day when her eyes landed on his handsome mug. His angry eyes glared her way as he stood before her.

"I told you that my mom did my pops like that. I didn't

meet him until I was fifteen. I don't like this type of shit. I'ma fuck with you later," he said and left the room.

Vadah fell back onto the bed and stared up at her ceiling. She thought of telling Quan daily, but she was scared. It was as simple as that. She wasn't only worried about how he would react but was fearful of how his kids and Tamm would take the news as well.

The next day, Vadah walked into the luncheon feeling refreshed. She'd had over six hours of sleep and was feeling fucking good. It showed on her pretty face that still held fat from her pregnancy weight. Her body had snapped back, and she now weighed a curvy 185 pounds. Vadah loved her added weight and welcomed the hair she'd grown as well from carrying her son.

As she walked through the crowded room in her black slacks that she'd paired with a soft pink blouse and black Fendi pumps, she thought of Jordyn. She hadn't spoken to her in months and really missed her.

They hadn't necessarily had a falling out, but they had disconnected, and she didn't like that. She made a mental note to call her girl and see how she was doing.

"Vadah!" Tamm yelled, running over.

Vadah turned at the sound of the voice she hadn't heard in way too long and was met with a glowing Tamm. Tamm's black hair hung to her shoulders while a black jumpsuit clung to her shapely frame. She hugged Vadah tightly as she rubbed her back.

"We missed you so much, boo. I came just to see if you would be here," Tamm confessed. "And I'm proud of all you've done," she said before letting her go.

Vadah's eyes watered as she peered back at Tamm. Tamm looked like a new woman.

"You're okay," Vadah murmured.

Tamm smiled brightly.

"I am. My crazy ass family and ex talked me into chemo,

and it killed the cancer. I've been holistic since then and look at me. I feel good, Vadah. Really good," Tamm emotionally replied.

Vadah hugged Tamm again and took her over to an empty table. Tamm smiled at Vadah as she wiped her eyes.

"Where is the baby? Your professor said you had a son," Tamm asked.

Vadah stopped smiling and cleared her throat. She sat up straight in her seat, and Tamm grinned at her.

"It's okay. When he told me that, I knew. I could feel it. My sister told me about him staying in your room, so it wasn't a shock to me. I'm just sorry I couldn't defuse the situation. I was very sick at the time, Vadah."

Vadah dropped her head. She stared at her lap as Tamm scooted her chair closer to her.

"Can I tell you a secret?" Tamm whispered.

Vadah nodded while breathing heavily.

"I wanted that to happen. I thought I was gonna die, and I wanted someone to love him and love my kids. I chose you for that, Vadah. I wasn't in love with him then, and I'm not in love with him now. We will only be friends for the rest of our lives. Don't stress over that because you didn't betray me, Vadah. You didn't," Tamm assured her and pulled Vadah into another hug.

Vadah cried softly as the weight lifted off her shoulders. She'd carried that pain around for months, fearing the day she saw Tamm and the truth about her son came out.

"I still feel bad, though. I was so stressed that I went into labor early. Thankfully he was fine and only stayed in the hospital for a few weeks before I could bring him home. Still just knowing what I had done rested heavily on my shoulders, Tamm. And hearing you say all of this is such a relief. But what will Morgan think?"

Tamm pulled back from the hug and smiled.

"Girl, she will be happy. I'm dating someone new, and

she's too busy hating him to hate you too. She always asks about you, and I know Ace can't wait to see you. When can we come over?"

Vadah shrugged.

"I don't know. I'm not ready to see Quan yet," she admitted.

Tamm nodded in understanding. She pulled a check from her purse and placed it on Vadah's lap. The $25,000 check was written out to Vadah's business in perfect penmanship.

"I understand, but he has a right to know. Promise you'll call me soon?"

Vadah clutched the check while smiling at Tamm.

"I promise I will," she replied and meant it.

Tamm hugged her again before leaving the luncheon.

CHAPTER

Fourteen

"*OHHH* GOD!"

Tye gritted his teeth. He slapped Jordyn on the ass before snatching up a handful of her long, red hair.

"Take it, take this dick, J," he demanded in his deep tone.

Jordyn whimpered. Her body went lax, and soon she was climaxing with Tye. They both fell onto the bed out of breath. Jordyn lazily wiped the sweat away from her forehead before pushing the muscular man off her. She glanced down at his sexy face and shook her head.

She'd met Ty'Shawn through his sister who modeled with her. He was cool. Older than her by six years, but she didn't mind. He took her mind away, spoiled her with the attention she craved, and when she dipped off on him, he allowed her to have her peace. He didn't hound her or blow up her phone with continuous phone calls like most the men she knew did. Tye was just a cool ass nigga, and she could fuck with that.

"You 'bout to dip?"

Jordyn smiled. Tye's gritty, deep voice always made her feel tingly on the inside.

"Don't I always? But this was nice. I just wanna lay in my own bed," she replied groggily.

Tye nodded. He liked Jordyn. Her pussy was right, clean, and always calling his name, but he refused to chase a bitch. He didn't give a damn who she was.

"That's what's up. Hit me up when you get that itch again. Okay?" he asked.

Jordyn got off his bed and looked at him. Sex had spread her hips. She was now thicker and had this sexiness to her that couldn't be ignored. He soaked in her beauty, wondering if she would ever let him entirely in.

"I will," she assured him, and only then could he relax and let sleep take him away.

Jordyn took a quick shower and re-dressed before leaving the hotel. As she pulled out of the parking lot, her mother called. In the last six months, she'd slowly pushed her family away. It wasn't that she didn't love them. Something like that would never be up for question. It was her.

Jordyn was the problem. Rome had abruptly left his home with his wife after her visit. Jordyn went crazy trying to find him. All the places he once visited were no longer places he stepped in, and it hurt. Jordyn tried to call Zion and talk with him about it, only to learn he'd blocked her. Once again Jordyn had been let down by a man.

Out of anger, she'd recklessly lost her virginity to a college basketball player one lonely night. He still called and tried to pursue her, but Jordyn wanted nothing more from him. He'd popped her cherry, and that was all she'd needed him to do.

Now that she was no longer a virgin, she fucked her pain away. It wasn't every man she saw, but she didn't keep count. She was safe with it, and their sex helped. Their kisses, their touches, soothed her temporarily until the pain returned. Jordyn was no longer in school, and if she didn't need the modeling to survive, she would have given that up as well.

"Yes, Mom," she answered in a bland tone.

Her mother, Logan, smacked her lips.

"You didn't call like you said you would."

Jordyn sighed. She was so sleepy and sore as fuck from sexing Tye all day.

"I was working."

Logan took a deep breath and exhaled.

"Jordyn. Baby talk to me. I know this has everything to do with Rome, and I'm sorry. Mommy is so sorry he hurt you. What did he do?" her mother asked in a weary tone.

Jordyn swallowed hard. *Gave me hope and snatched that shit away. I wasn't even worth a phone call to him.*

"Nothing. I said I would come down for Toni's party. I wasn't lying. I will," she replied with an attitude.

Her mom sniffled into the phone.

"I'm hurting too, Jordyn. We all are. We love you, and we're worried. I can't watch you self-destruct," Logan said before falling apart on the phone.

Jordyn, no longer able to hear her mother's cries, ended the call. She drove to her new apartment that was located in downtown Royal Oak, and she went into her place. Jordyn stripped out of her clothes and turned on some Tamia.

Another one of her faves.

Jordyn sat on her sofa as the music filled the room, and she sparked up her joint. As the song began to play, she smoked her troubles away.

All I hear is raindrops
  Falling on the rooftop
  Oh, baby tell me why'd you have to go
  Cause this pain I feel
  It won't go away
  And today I'm officially missing you

The words. The things they meant to Jordyn made her cry. She pulled her knees up to her chest as she wept.

"I hate you, Rome. I fucking hate you for not loving me," she whispered. She finished her weed before dozing off to sleep.

Two days later, Jordyn stepped off the plane at Hartsfield International Airport. Atlanta felt good. So many childhood memories ran through her mind as she walked through the packed airport.

Her summers that she'd spent with her family. Her high school years, even the friends she no longer answered the phone for, she briefly missed.

"Jordyn!" Toni, her younger sister shrieked, running her way.

Toni was ten. Jordyn and Bellamy Jr. always joked and said she was the *oops* baby, although they would never tell her that. Jordyn hugged her beautiful sister tightly. Toni always made her feel like she could save the world. She was already following in Jordyn's footsteps by doing a few modeling jobs. Logan just didn't want her little red-haired beauty to get lost in the glitz and glamour, so she made sure that Toni always put her studies first.

"I missed you, Jordy," Toni whispered with her eyes watering.

"We all did, sis," Bellamy Jr. said as he walked up.

Beside him was the rest of their family. It had been months since they'd laid eyes on Jordyn, so yes, the whole crew showed up to bring her home. Only person missing was her Aunt Kolbee who was out of town.

"Jordyn come here. Let me see you," Logan said as she slowly approached her daughter.

They looked like sisters instead of mother and daughter. Jordyn had gotten her reddish-orange hair from her mother's side of the family along with her freckles. Her eyes were from her dad, whose mother had light colored peepers.

"You're thicker. You've also been drinking soda. Your face is breaking out, and you haven't had much sleep. Weed must have had your mind racing," Logan assumed while appraising Jordyn like only a mother could.

Jordyn dropped her shoulders because it was all true, and Logan pulled her into a hug.

"It'll be okay," Logan quietly promised her.

After hugging Bezo, the family of five got into Bezo's G-Wagon and went to get something to eat. While Toni talked Jordyn's ear off about everything that she'd missed, the rest of the family stared at Jordyn's new appearance. Jordyns skin was now decorated with tattoos. **Fuck Love** was in cursive along Jordyn's left collarbone. Latin scriptures lined the inside of her right arm, while a dead sunflower rested on top of her right shoulder.

Logan saw the signs. All the things that she'd gone through behind having issues with her father, and she shook her head. Looking at Jordyn was like staring in a mirror.

"Your granny and Jerricka said you blocked them. What's up with that?" her mom asked, breaking the silence.

Jordyn looked at her mother and licked her chapped lips. She was already yearning for some weed. She needed the medicinal relief to clear her thoughts.

"I did," she mumbled as she shuffled the food around the plate.

Logan cleared her throat as Bezo lovingly rubbed her thigh.

"Jordyn Flint, why would you do that?"

To block out the noise.

Jordyn shrugged. Logan went to speak, and Bellamy Jr. cut her off.

"Remember when we went to Atlantis with Toni for the first time, and you farted loud as hell in front of everyone by accident? That was funny," he said, and Jordyn nodded, remembering the vacation.

The staring match she was having with her mother was unnerving.

"Your eyes are sunken in. You're dressed like a damn bum. Your grades are shitty as hell, and you're acting like a zombie. You're coming home," her mother said while glaring her way.

Jordyn shook her head. She was grown, and she refused to let her mother run her life.

"Calm down, baby. Jordyn, maybe you should come back just for a while," Bezo interjected.

Jordyn shook her head again. They didn't get it. She wasn't coming back to Atlanta to live anytime soon. She'd created a life in Detroit, and she liked it there.

"No, I won't. I take care of myself. I'm grown," she replied with a shrug.

Logan's eyes bucked at her daughter.

"Are you? You look like shit! You should be graduating college not modeling for Instagram boutiques. You could be so much more, Jordyn. Why are you doing this to yourself?" her mom angrily asked.

The people in the five-star restaurant stared their way. The fancy french style bistro restaurant wasn't used to so much ruckus, and their small spat was causing a scene.

"Let's go," Bezo said, not wanting their business to end up on a blog.

People were known for selling stories about him whether it was real or fake.

"Why can't you just let me live my life?" Jordyn asked, standing to her feet.

Her mom looked at her worriedly, and briefly, she felt guilt. Jordyn shook her head as she refused to back down. The last thing she wanted to do was return home. She had so much unfinished business in Detroit that it wasn't even funny.

"Because it's my job to stop you before you run into the wall," her mom said and walked off.

Back at home, a place Jordyn felt like she hadn't been to in forever, she lay on her brother's bed as he rolled up a blunt. A towel sat at the foot of his door as both of the windows in his room were opened.

"You really in some janky shit. You went from saying we both had a plan, to you saying fuck it all on some Elsa shit."

Jordyn laughed. She looked at her little brother who was now a young man and sighed. He was tall, and the gym he used regularly had him sporting muscles and shit. A small beard sat on his face, and his short hair was cut into a fade. He was just as handsome as his father.

"I'm not perfect. I don't know why the hell you all keep trying to make me be that way. I have flaws. A bunch of them."

Bellamy Jr. nodded.

"Shit, I know, but the people who love you, me, mom, and my pops, we going through it too. This shit is not just affecting you, Jordyn. It's selfish to me at this point what you're doing and shit. I listened to mom cry for hours about you, and you sitting up here mad. Fuck you mad at? We the ones who should be mad at you. I know your real dad not shit. I can see you hurt behind it but look at everything you still was blessed with. You could be down real bad right now, but you not. And one some real shit, the stuff you doing now is because you choosing to do it. It's like you addicted to the pain, sis," Bellamy Jr. said bluntly while looking her way.

Jordyn stared up at the ceiling in deep thought. Her brother, who was wise beyond his years, had given it to her raw with no chaser. Her first reaction was to cut into him until she really thought about what he said. Jordyn pulled her bottom lip into her mouth and asked herself. Was she addicted to the pain?

Am I though?

After spending a week with her family, Jordyn was on her last day in Atlanta. She'd been at the spa for most of the day with her mom and auntie Kolbee. Kolbee was her twin in so many ways. She looked more like her aunt than her own mom, and they did possess a special bond. Kolbee was also hurt that Jordyn had been evading her phone calls.

"I'm serious. You call me whenever you need me, niece. Okay?"

Jordyn looked at Kolbee, feeling greater than she'd felt in months.

"I will. I love you and tell Denali I said hi."

Kolbee nodded and hugged her again. Jordyn joined her mom in the locker room, and they got dressed. Logan took Jordyn to her father's gravesite. Logan's father was a man by the name of Deron Flint. He was well known throughout a few cities and eventually made Atlanta his home.

Logan had gone through astronomical changes behind her father and his choice to make another child, her sister, Kolbee, with a woman who wasn't her mother. That one act had altered four lives forever.

As Logan and Jordyn sat against Deron's headstone, Logan pulled her daughter to her side. Despite what they looked like, she was the mother, and Jordyn was her daughter. Logan didn't care if she had a hundred kids, Jordyn would always be her baby. Her first born, the little girl who stole her heart the moment she entered the earth.

"I'm sorry, Momma. I know it's wrong to push you guys away, but sometimes I hurt so bad that I just want to be left alone," Jordyn whispered, feeling bad.

Logan sighed as she rubbed her daughter's arm.

"I know. I know how it feels, baby. My parents didn't work out, and my daddy left. My mom couldn't accept Auntie Kolbee for a very long time. It was hard for her to, and she hated him. Her hate rubbed off on me, and for years, I hated him too. I was mad at him, then I met your father, and we just couldn't make it work. He didn't make me happy like I hoped he would, so I broke things off with him. He was mad at me for that, baby. He stopped taking my calls and seeing you. Even when he did, it wasn't long, and he was angry. Very bitter," Logan exclaimed, and for some reason, Zion popped into Jordyn's mind.

Jordyn shook her head to rid him from her thoughts. He wasn't fucking with her, and she needed to accept that.

"I battled with Rome. I battled with my dad. I didn't trust men. I hated them, and I used them solely for sex. My father, your grandfather, was a good man, baby. He loved Auntie Kolbee and me so much. It took me going through a lot of pain to realize that. I wasted good years. Time me nor your aunt can ever get back."

Jordyn peered curiously up at her mom.

"You was mad at Auntie Kolbee too?"

Logan nodded while smiling.

"Yeah. Shit, in my eyes, she was the devil. She was taking my daddy away from me. Our mommas even battled it out. We were all hurt. Tasia handled it better than all of us, but I'm sure she felt the pain when she saw how sad Kolbee was for being pushed to the side. Much how you feel, right?"

Jordyn nodded solemnly.

"Yeah," she whispered.

"When you're feeling like this, you need to express it. All this pushing us away stuff stops today. I won't let years go by where we don't see you. Yes, I'm upset about your school, but I'm more worried about *you*. You're my daughter. Fuck that college. I need Jordyn to be okay for Jordyn. I would go insane if something were to happen to you. Do you under-stand that?" Logan asked and sniffled.

Jordyn nodded with her own eyes watering.

"This family is going to be on you like white on rice. When you get home, you will regularly see and spend time with your granny and Jerricka. Even hang with your friend Vadah. You haven't talked about her in months. How is she doing?" her mom asked.

Jordyn shrugged, feeling like a bad friend. She'd seen

online that Vadah had started her business and had a baby. She was proud of her girl, but with so much pain in her life, she hadn't made any attempts to see her.

"She's doing really good now, ma. She stopped doing videos and went back to school. She even had a baby, and it didn't stop her," Jordyn replied proudly.

Her mom smiled.

"That's good, baby. That's what you need. To be around someone that's headed somewhere. Have you spoken with Zion?"

Jordyn quickly shook her head, and her mom shrugged while staring at her.

"It's his loss, baby," her mother said as Rome's mother slowly approached the grave with flowers.

She'd met Deron, of course, when Jordyn was just a baby, and he'd seemed like a sweet man. She was nervous. She hadn't spoken to or seen her grandbaby in so long, and she wasn't sure how Jordyn would feel about their reuniting.

"Jordyn, this is your grandmother Katie," Logan said and stood up.

Her past with Katie was jaded. Katie had even held physical encounters with Logan's mom behind Jordyn and how bad Rome was doing her. It left the two families at war, and sadly, Jordyn had paid the price.

"Hi sweetie, my God, she's beautiful," Katie expressed before hugging Logan.

Katie squeezed Logan tightly and shook her head. She had so many regrets and cutting off Jordyn was her biggest one. "I'm sorry, Logan. We, the family, are so sorry," she whispered.

Logan nodded. She didn't understand it. She wouldn't pretend to because she could never stop being around someone she loved, blood-related or not, but for Jordyn, she would accept the apology. Her baby needed this to move forward. Whether it worked out or not, Jordyn needed this closure.

Logan could see that without it, her daughter might only get worse.

"Jordyn, you look so beautiful," Katie said, staring back at Jordyn with eyes that resembled hers.

Katie was black, and her family was from New Orleans. They were known for their fair skin and emerald colored eyes.

"Thank you," Jordyn shyly said.

Katie pulled Jordyn into a hug and held her tightly. Her next words were almost too much to say, but they needed to be said. Katie had spoken with Logan. She heard about her granddaughter's troubles, and she had voiced all of them to Rome. He responded, and this was what he said.

"He's scared, Jordyn. Your father made a lot of mistakes with you, and he's afraid to face you. He won't man up," Katie said and rubbed her nose. She let Jordyn go and grabbed the tops of her shoulders. Katie had been in Atlanta for the last two years, and every day that passed, she prayed that she'd cross paths with Jordyn just to see her pretty face.

"That's on him, baby. Don't let his mistakes, alter your future. You will find your purpose in life and live it. That's with or without your father involved. I love my son, but he has failed you, baby. I have as well, and I'm sorry. I don't want you to wait for an apology from him that may never come.

"We don't always get the answer to every question that we have in life. Sometimes we have to accept what's right in front of us, and that fact is your father is not who he should be for you. He didn't raise you, and he didn't love you like you needed and wanted, Jordyn. He was selfish, and you deserved better. That came in the form of your mother's husband. Shame on Rome. Shame on him," Katie said and started to cry.

CHAPTER

Fifteen

Her feet felt heavy as bricks as she walked up a walkway that she hadn't ventured up in months. The lawn was decorated differently while newer cars sat in the driveway. The front door was cracked as balloons covered the glass double doors. She smiled as she remembered that purple and white were Morgan's favorite colors.

Adir smiled as she carried him while also carrying his diaper bag and a gift bag.

"Here goes nothing," she mumbled as she slowly stepped through the doors.

Kids' laughter and the smell of popcorn greeted Vadah as she walked slowly down the hall. The jeans she'd worn were a bit too tight while the top she wore had her breasts spilling out of them. She needed to breastfeed her son before the milk spilled into her bra.

"Vadah!" Morgan yelled as she rounded the corner.

In the sunken family room was close to twenty people. The conversation seemed to stop as Morgan ran toward

Vadah. She hugged her leg tightly, and Adir stirred in Vadah's arms. Morgan peered up at him curiously and smiled. In the last year, she'd grown so much.

"Can I hold him?" she innocently asked.

Vadah nodded. Her eyes did a brief scan of the room and landed on Tamm's sister Teresa. She sat on the loveseat with a deep scowl on her face. Vadah smiled at her, anxious to repay her for the ass whooping before looking back down to Morgan.

"Yes, right after I feed him."

"Everyone, this is Vadah. She's family," Tamm said and walked over to Vadah.

Tamm looked radiant in a Versace printed pantsuit with her hair in soft waves. She gently grabbed Adir and peered lovingly down at him.

"Welcome to the family, little guy. You look just like your daddy," she cooed holding him securely in her arms.

A few people smiled as Teresa stood up. Vadah dropped the bags, wanting to be ready the second time around, and Tamm shook her head.

"Teresa, this is my home. If you don't like how I run things, you can leave and don't forget to take your negative spirit with you," Tamm said without bothering to look at her baby sister.

Teresa snarled. She snatched up her Balmain fanny pack and rushed past Tamm and Vadah. Tamm smiled at Vadah as she gently rocked Adir in her arms.

"You can feed him in Ace's nursery. Ace and his father went to the store, so you have a few minutes before it hits the fan," she said and passed Adir back.

Vadah nodded and moved swiftly to Ace's nursery. The room was now changed into a new nursery space with new furniture and decor. Vadah's jaw dropped as she read Adir's name across the back wall.

"Please don't think I'ma creep. I just figured that he could stay over whenever you were comfortable with it. I can watch him," Tamm said from the doorway.

Vadah sat in the rocker facing the door and took out her left breast. Immediately, Adir latched on and started feeding. She looked at Tamm and noticed she was wearing an engagement ring.

"You let me watch your kids, so of course, you can watch mine. I'm shocked at how accepting you are, but I swear I appreciate it. I didn't want any drama with you, Tamm."

Tamm waved her off and stepped to the side as Ace charged into the room. He was taller, had shed some pounds, and was grinning like only a happy kid could. He ran over to Vadah and tried to climb onto her leg. Vadah's heart warmed as she realized that he hadn't forgotten her.

"Aye chill out. You don't wanna knock your baby brother down," Quan said when he walked into the room.

Vadah's heart stopped at his words. The sound of his deep voice made her body slightly shake. She slowly raised her head, and her eyes connected with his. His amber gaze that matched her son's seared into her as he stood next to Tamm.

"Please don't be mad, but he asked who this was for, and I told him. I'll leave you all alone," Tamm said and grabbed Ace.

Ace whined as she carried him out of the room. Tamm closed the door behind herself, and Quan chose to lean against the door. He watched Vadah intently as she breastfed their son.

"You know this shit is damn near unforgivable," he said lowly.

Vadah switched breasts, and Adir cupped her chest. His eyes closed as he continued to get her milk. She peered up at Quan and swallowed hard. Quan was bigger, but it suited him. His small belly poked out of his designer polo style black tee that had white lettering on the front. He wore black jeans with Yeezy sneakers and a black Rolex. As he scratched at his small chin hairs, he glared at Vadah.

"You don't have shit to say? I called you for months. Even popped up at the fucking condo, and not once did you tell me about this shit. What the fuck!" he raged, and Adir began to cry.

Vadah sighed as she picked her son up. She rubbed his back as Quan walked over to them. He grabbed Adir from her arms and held him like only a seasoned father could. Immediately, Adir calmed down as Quan peered down at him.

"I'm getting a test," he lowly declared.

Vadah rolled her eyes. Quan was beginning to piss her off.

"Whatever."

Quan nodded.

"Tamm told me you was back in school and doing good with your business. I'm happy to see shit worked out for you, but now you need to mentally grow up. When you fuck up, admit the shit and learn from it. I'ma hold on to lil dude for a while," he said and left the room.

Two days later, Vadah walked through Allure Boutique with Jordyn. She was elated to finally be catching up with her girl. They'd both been through so much over the last year and was glad to be in each other's presence. While Vadah wore workout gear, Jordyn was clad in an acid blue leggings outfit that she wore clear mules with. Both women wore their hair in its natural state as they walked through the upscale boutique.

"So, he still has Adir?"

Vadah solemnly nodded. She'd been shacked up at Quan's downtown Detroit penthouse with her son. Quan had taken the DNA test and was awaiting the results to what they both knew.

"Yes, and it put me in a messed-up position. Jase has been calling me nonstop. I texted him yesterday and told him that I finally told Quan, and I think he got mad at me. He was one of the people pushing me to tell Quan in the first fucking place," Vadah griped.

Jordyn shook her head.

"I thought I was going through it. I see your ass was too. I can't believe you have a baby, and by Quan at that. Then you got back with Jase's old cheating ass," Jordyn quipped, making them both snicker.

Vadah shoulder bumped Jordyn, and Jordyn smiled at her.

"No, but seriously, are you still in love with Jase?"

Vadah shrugged. She was, but it wasn't as strong as what she felt for Quan.

"I have love for Jase. I think after I was finally able to leave him alone the first time, I told myself to never fall that deep in love with him again. However, he's been there for me. He helped a lot when I was pregnant, and he helps me out now, but neither of us is lying to each other. We both still carry the friend title, and we haven't had sex," Vadah revealed.

"Well, shit, you good, then. You can continue to let him know how you're feeling, and he can decide if he wanna battle it out with Quan for your heart. At least you have Quan back in your life. Maybe it's meant for you two to be together. Tamm is cool with it, and you're in a much better space. Your stars are aligned," Jordyn replied.

Vadah nodded. She didn't fuck with that astrology shit like that, but if that was the case, she wouldn't complain. She picked up a few shirts before peering over at Jordyn.

"You seem better. But are you really good now?"

Jordyn nodded as she placed two pairs of gold hoops into her basket.

"I am. It took me a while, no lie, to get my shit right. My real dad up and disappeared on me, and Zion cut me off. I was down bad out here, girl. Damn near suicidal. You were right when you said I was putting too much into him. I'd placed all my happiness on Zion, and when he walked away, I was lost. I started fucking up in school and having sex. I'ma keep it real with you," Jordyn said and cleared her throat.

"I was running through some niggas. I wasn't letting them run no trains or nothing like that, but I was hitting whoever I wanted. My parents had me fly down to Atlanta for my sister's birthday, and it was the break I needed to reflect. I saw how hurt everyone was because of me, and it was a wakeup call. I was self-destructive, Vadah. My parents put me in counseling, and I'm doing okay. Everyday isn't rainbows and glitter, but I feel better. I don't wake up feeling like I need a dick up in me to cope," she replied.

Vadah stopped walking to look at Jordyn. She hated that her friend had gone through so much alone.

"I'm sorry I wasn't there for you, and I'm glad to see you're trying to heal. I know it's a process, but at least you've started it. I started back talking with my dad, and it helped me out a lot. To see that your dad still is on that bullshit makes me appreciate my father so much more. I know you are hurting because of him, but don't forget about the good father God did bless you with," Vadah told her and smiled.

Jordyn nodded with wet lenses. She rubbed at the tip of her nose as she licked her lips.

"I haven't, and I won't. I've neglected him for a while now because of Rome, but trust, I'm done with that ungrateful shit. I'm only loving the people who are loving me. We gotta be there for the ones who always had our back. We gone' get our shit together, Vadah. This broken shit isn't a good look for us," Jordyn jested, and Vadah snorted.

"Hell no, it's not. Fuck a broken heart and a broken spirit. I'm trying to see what that healed life is looking like," Vadah said, and they both laughed.

"Shit, me too. I wanna know what that life be like," Jordyn said before they finished shopping in the store.

After leaving the boutique, Vadah met up with Jase at his

clothing store. Jase sold designer threads and had two loca-tions. Vadah was proud of all he'd accomplished and loved how determined he was to make something of himself.

As Jase talked with one of his employees by the front of his store, Vadah stared at him. There was no comparing Jase to Quan. They were two different men. While Quan was tall, standing at 6'5" Jase was six feet even. Jase was a few shades darker than Quan and held a more hood look to him. Jase rocked an even fade with a trimmed beard. He was always wearing Timbs or Jordan's and had a relaxed style to him. He was a chill nigga, and that was one thing Vadah felt he did have in common with Quan.

She licked her lips as she headed Jase's way.

"What's up?" he asked, pulling her into a hug.

Vadah shook her head. She hugged him tightly as his worker quietly stepped away. Jase peered down at her and stared into her eyes as he held her.

"You coming in here to break my heart?"

He laughed, but Vadah felt the seriousness in his tone. She sighed and broke the gaze.

"I'm just coming to check on you. I felt like you was upset with me for being at his place."

Jase rubbed her back before letting her go. He grabbed her hand and led her into his office. As Vadah sat on the leather black sofa near his right wall he sat on the edge of his desk.

"I wanted you to let him know about Adir, but I wasn't expecting you to shack up with the nigga after that. Yeah, we do this friends shit, Vadah, but let me be clear 'bout some shit. I don't wanna be your fucking friend. I wanna be your man, ma. That's why I'm here," Jase replied.

Vadah rubbed the back of her neck. She could feel the temperature in the room rise at his declaration.

"But you don't feel the same way," Jase noted and stood up. He fixed his diamond bezel watch and slowly nodded. Vadah felt like shit as she watched him run both of his hands over his fade. "So, I was the backup nigga? Is this payback for me cheating on you in the past?"

Vadah quickly shook her head.

"No, I wouldn't do that. I'm not even cut like that, Jase. I do care for you, but I'm just dealing with a lot right now. You know that, and this has nothing to do with Quan. I'm not with him and not trying to be. I just need to keep focusing on me and Adir."

Jase walked over to Vadah and dropped to his knees. He peered up into her eyes, and she smiled at him.

"Then shit don't have to change with us," he said and grabbed her face. "As long as you not fucking him, we good," he said and kissed her sensually.

CHAPTER
Sixteen

"YOU LOOK GOOD, BABY," Tye said as he looked Jordyn over.

Jordyn smiled. He wasn't Zion, but he would do. She was trying to change for the better and taking everything one day at a time. She'd been writing out her feelings and had somehow ended up with a book of songs that she was thinking about selling to a deserving singer. As she felt better mentally, she felt it was only right for her to start back enjoying life, so she was with Tye and Vadah at one of Tye's popular Detroit strip clubs.

Jordyn nor Vadah had stepped out in a while, so they were dressed in their Sunday best, garnering more attention than the dancers. While Vadah rocked a neon lime colored midi dress with black Fendi heels, Jordyn was decked out in an emerald green criss cross back frill hem shift dress that clung to her shapely body. Jordyn wore her hair wild and curly while Vadah rocked a silk press.

Both women tossed money, Tye's money, to be exact at the sexy dancers as Tye and his boys filled up the large VIP section.

"Tye is fine, bitch," Vadah whispered and tossed some twenties at the dancer in front of her.

Jordyn giggled. She hit the blunt again and assessed Tye. He was sexy, with his smooth, peanut hued brown skin. Tye was tall with a lean build. He rocked his hair in a burst fade with the tips of his curly hair dyed a light brown. His face was boyishly handsome, making him look younger than he was. He housed full lips with slanted eyes and a straight nose. Tye normally wore designer shit from head to toe and was always flossing his diamond chains that Jordyn knew for a fact were real.

He was flashy at times, but she didn't care. She wasn't trying to wife him. She simply loved his dick game better than the other niggas calling her phone, so for the moment, he had her attention.

"He's cool," she murmured, and Tye peered over at her. Jordyn blew him a kiss, and he walked her way. "Chill with your boys! Don't be coming over here bugging me, nigga," she joked as he hugged her from the back.

"Shit fuck them niggas. I would much rather be in your space. Why you so fucking fine, Jordyn? Huh?" he asked and kissed her neck.

Jordyn blushed as Vadah winked at her.

"You'll have to thank my momma for that. I look just like her."

Tye snorted.

"Well shit, were she at? I want her ass too. I can handle both of y'all." He laughed, only Jordyn didn't join in with him.

She frowned as she slowly pulled away. Tye slapped her ass, and she glared back at him.

"That wasn't funny. Me nor my mom get down like that. Don't joke with me like I'm one of your hoes, Tye. Go chill with your boys and get the fuck out of my face," she snapped.

Tye nodded. He rubbed her ass one last time before

walking off. Jordyn walked back over to Vadah and watched Tye pull a dancer onto his lap from the corner of her eye. Tye was cool, but his slick ass comment didn't sit well with her.

"That nigga just pissed me off. Talking about he wants me and my momma. I almost slapped his goofy looking ass," Jordyn grumbled.

Vadah laughed as she tossed her last twenty to a dark-skinned dancer with a bubble butt and pretty face.

"Oh, he tried it. You must have pulled the old Jordyn out on him because he's scared to even look over here at you right now," Vadah noted.

Jordyn nodded, suddenly ready to go. Since counseling, she'd been trying to release her pain in healthy ways, and while Tye wasn't harmful to her, she did still use him for a sexual purpose. She bit her lip as she pondered if it was time to let Tye with his big old dick go.

Jordyn stuck around the club for another hour before Vadah tugged on her arm. Vadah's eyes widened as she looked at her.

"Quan is here. They just announced the shit, so that means we gotta go. Come on," she said hurriedly and walked off.

Jordyn smiled as she headed for Tye. He was high as fuck as he sat on the sofa next to a pretty dancer. The dancer smiled at Jordyn before turning her attention to Tye's homeboy.

"Hey! I'm about to go. You should be leaving too. You're fucked up," she yelled, standing over him.

Tye smirked up at Jordyn and licked his lips.

"You not coming with me? I know you not still mad about earlier. I done fucked plenty of mothers and daughters together. That shit ain't that deep," he replied and closed his eyes.

Jordyn bit down hard on her bottom lip. Instead of slapping the shit out of Tye, she exited his VIP section. She found Vadah leaving the club with her head down. Vadah was on the phone arguing as they handed over their ticket for valet.

Seconds later, Vadah's Beamer pulled up, and they slid in. Vadah put her phone away and glanced over at Jordyn.

"He's crazy as shit, Jordyn. I can't deal with him. Now that he knows Adir is his, he thinks he can run my life. That same controlling shit like before when I was working with him, and it's driving me insane. He actually asked me why I didn't tell him I was at the club? Like I need his fucking permission to go out. He has me fucked up," Vadah grumbled.

Jordyn relaxed in her seat. She nodded as she gazed out of the window. Her high had worn off, and she was sleepy.

"Niggas will be niggas. Quan will only do what you allow him to do, Vadah. Are you still at his place?"

Vadah shook her head.

"Girl, I think that nigga is following us! My God, he's gonna make me act a fool on his tall ass," she vented and pulled into the closest gas station parking lot.

Vadah parked near an empty pump, and seconds later, a matte orange Lamborghini truck pulled behind them. Quan jumped out of the truck, and Vadah rolled down her window.

Jordyn leaned over and took a glance at the man who she knew her friend was in love with as he leaned down into the car. His amber eyes seared angrily into them as he stared their way.

"Where is Adir? Why the fuck are you at the strip club? That clubbing shit is not a good look for you," he complained.

Vadah shook her head, and Quan assessed her outfit. His eyes widened as he opened her car door.

"What do you have on? What the fuck is this shit? You out looking for a nigga?" he angrily asked.

Vadah nodded, and Jordyn had to force herself to not laugh.

"I believe I am. One who knows I am a grown ass woman

and not his child. One who's considerate of my needs and my time," Vadah replied seriously.

Quan chuckled.

"You won't find that nigga at the titty bar. Come here real quick, Vadah," he said and pulled her out of the car.

Jordyn sighed as she imagined herself in the bed. Vadah's soap opera shit was for the birds. She was fucking tired.

Jordyn pulled out her cell phone and wrote down various song lyrics that wouldn't leave her brain until a light tap on the window garnered her attention. She looked up, and her eyes connected with Zion's.

Jordyn didn't know how to feel as she lowered the window. As if it was possible, he looked better than he did the last time she'd seen him. He wore black jeans with a red Billionaire Boys t-shirt and a black Detroit fitted. His eyes, those intriguing dark orbs of his were at peace. She no longer saw trouble brewing in them, and for him, she was happy. Still, the way he'd cut her off had her giving him an icy greeting.

"Vadah said you was in the car, and I had to call bullshit. It's been a while, ma," he coolly said.

Jordyn nodded. Her phone vibrated, and she noticed Tye was calling her. Zion noticed her phone was ringing as well, and he licked his lips. She was beautiful; he would be a fool to think he was the only one enamored by her beauty. He was smart enough to know that wasn't the case.

"That's your man?" he probed with his eyes on her.

Jordyn shook her head. She stared down at her lap, not ready to talk with the nigga who had abruptly cut her off, and he leaned into the car. His scent infiltrated the space around her as he lightly pecked her cheek.

"You're still beautiful as hell. I missed you," he confessed huskily.

Jordyn started to breathe hard. She was still struggling

with moving ahead and wasn't sure if Zion popping back up in her life was a good or a bad thing.

Zion opened the car door and pulled her out of the car. He pulled her into his arms and hugged her tightly. Jordyn's silence was fucking him up. It had been moments in the past when he couldn't get her to shut up.

"I'm sorry about dipping out on you. I had to get my shit together," he apologized.

Jordyn swallowed hard before nodding. Vadah walked back over with a calmer Quan on her heels as Zion stared down at Jordyn.

"Hey, we can go," Vadah said before getting into her car.

Jordyn nodded and pushed back from Zion. She looked up at him and gave him half a smile.

"It's cool. I'm used to it, but I'm glad to see you're doing better," she replied.

Jordyn got into the car with Vadah as Quan stuck his face in the car.

"Can you meet me at my place? Or I can come to yours, what's good?" he politely asked.

Jordyn smiled to herself. He was acting like a new nigga.

"I don't think so. My mom has Adir. I plan on picking him up early tomorrow and going to church."

Quan sighed.

"And me and the kids would like to do that with y'all too. Can we?" he asked and whispered something into Vadah's ear.

Vadah started her car as she looked straight ahead.

"Maybe next week," she replied, and Quan's shoulders fell.

"Alright," he grumbled before walking off.

Zion looked longingly at Jordyn as she sat in the car.

"Can I call you?"

Jordyn snorted. Now he wanted to call her? Nah, she was good on that.

"That won't be necessary, but it was good seeing you," Jordyn replied, and Vadah pulled away before Zion could say anything else.

Jordyn relaxed in her seat as Zion plagued her mind. She thought of all the good times they'd shared and swallowed hard. One of the hardest things she had to do was tell him no, when all she really wanted to do was scream yes so they could get back to how they were before. However, Zion had already walked out on her once, and she wasn't trying to see if he would do it again.

Seventeen

"OPEN UP."

Vadah held tightly onto her robe. She'd just stepped out of the shower and was angry to see that Quan hadn't taken his ass home. Instead, he was pounding on her door.

Vadah waited a few minutes to see if he would leave, and he began to knock loudly again. She groaned as she pulled the door open. His amber eyes lustfully gazed down at her as he walked through the door.

"Why are you over here?"

Quan locked up behind himself and slipped off his sneakers. He dropped his chains onto Vadah's side table and pulled off his shirt. Vadah turned before he could get completely naked and walked into her bedroom.

"I could have had somebody here, Quan. You don't have the right to pop up at my shit. You don't pay the fucking rent, I do," she griped.

Quan walked up behind Vadah and tugged on her robe. His warm breath smelled of cognac as he leaned down to kiss her neck. Sensually, his hands caressed her soft breasts.

"Do you believe in fate?" he asked while rubbing on her nipples.

Milk began to slip from her areolas, and Vadah groaned. Quan ignored the liquid sliding down her breasts as he kissed her neck.

"I need to pump," she moaned.

Quan shook his head. While hugging her from the back, he led her into the bathroom. Vadah's breathing picked up as he toyed with her sensitive nipples.

"I think it's fate that has us here right now, Vadah. I'm still pissed at you for hiding my son, and you hate my attitude, but that's not enough for either of us to say fuck each other. Is it?" he asked and spun her around.

Vadah stared down at Quan as he began to suck on her nipples. She was embarrassed by her leakage, but he didn't seem to mind as he sucked on her pebbled areolas. Her head fell back as two of his fingers filled her sex. Slowly, he slid them in and out of her until she climaxed on his fingers. Quan then carried a naked Vadah into the shower and turned it on. His clothes had been discarded, and as he hoisted Vadah up, the hot water began to spray against their skin.

"Don't hide nothing else from me, and I'll work on my attitude. Okay?"

Vadah gazed into his eyes as she held onto him tightly. Slowly, his thick member slipped inside of her, and her body shuddered. She hadn't had sex since the last time she'd done it with him.

"Okay," she whispered as he sensually pounded into her.

Quan grunted before licking her top and bottom lip.

"As soon as you cum, I want you to call that nigga who left them dingy ass Timbs over here and tell his ass it's a wrap. Okay?"

Vadah nodded while grinning at him. Quan sucked his teeth as he pulled his member back. He roughly thrust back into Vadah, and her eyes closed in pleasure. She shuddered as he worked her pussy over in the shower.

"I'll tell him!" she shrieked, on the verge of cumming.

Quan ignored her cries of pleasure as he pounded her sex out while the water beat against their skin.

Hours later, Vadah rested peacefully in her bed. Small, sticky hands rubbed on her face as she snored slightly. The hands then yanked on her hair before she heard laughter. Vadah opened her eyes and smiled groggily at Ace. She pulled up the sheet over her naked frame as Ace sat in the bed with her. He ate his candy while grinning at her.

"I missed you, and why are you eating candy? It's too early for that."

"Ma, it's almost five o'clock," Quan said as he walked into the room carrying Adir.

Vadah looked over at Quan and sighed. He was dressed down in Nike sweats, and somehow, Ace and Adir wore matching clothing with him. She shook her head as she realized that his dick had knocked her ass out.

"Wow, I don't know what to say," she admitted, still sleepy.

Quan grabbed her phone off the dresser and tossed it onto the bed.

"I do. Call up that nigga and tell him you not available," he replied.

Vadah frowned as Ace tried to hand her his candy.

"I'm good, baby, you can eat it. And Quan, what do you mean I'm not available? I am single. What we did last night doesn't change that."

Quan walked over to the bed and sat down. His eyes peered down at Vadah as he held their son.

"I'm too old to be playing these games. I'm letting you know right now that I wanna see what we could be. Like before I'm all in. If you not with that shit, then let me know, and I'll fall back. But if you are, you need to call that nigga and cut his ass off. It's as simple as that," he replied.

Vadah chewed her bottom lip as she grabbed her cell. She

unlocked it and called up Jase. He immediately took the call as music played in his background.

"I thought you was hitting up church with a nigga. What happened to you?" he asked.

Vadah swallowed hard. She looked up and noticed Quan staring right at her. She broke his gaze as she smiled at Ace.

"I overslept. I needed to talk to you about us though, Jase. I really appreciate all that you did while I was pregnant and even after that. You've changed in so many ways—"

"Aye, I see where this shit going, and it's all good. I hope shit works out for you, Vadah. If you need me for anything, just hit me up," Jase replied and ended the call.

Vadah set her phone down and Quan licked his lips.

"Did you love him?" he asked.

Vadah snorted.

"If I did, I wouldn't have done that. He was good to me, though. Where is Morgan?"

Quan laid Adir down on the bed and rubbed Vadah's leg.

"With Tamm. They in Chicago with Tamm's fiancé. Morgan didn't want to go, but she be giving the nigga the blues, so I made her ass go. I'll bring her over when Tamm gets back. I wouldn't pursue you to hurt you. I wanna be with you, and that was before I found out about Adir. I won't hurt you if that's what you thinking," he told her.

Vadah nodded. She believed that he wouldn't as well. He didn't come off as that type.

"I believe you, but still, I'm scared. My heart has been broken more than a few times. First by my dad then Jase. It also broke when I had to walk away from you. I can't take another heartache, Quan."

Quan leaned over and pecked her lips before picking up Adir. Ace climbed off the bed and began to pull open Vadah's dresser drawers as Quan stared at her.

"And you won't have to suffer one. I know what I want,

and it's you. Like I told you before, ma, I see nothing but good shit happening for us. Come here," he lowly demanded.

Vadah sat up with the sheet pulled close to her body, and Quan kissed her lips. She peered into his eyes as he kissed her once more.

"I promise on my life, you'll be good with me. I just wanna make you happy," he declared and kissed her again.

THREE WEEKS LATER, Jordyn walked out of her counseling session feeling good. Every day that she woke up, she put forth a genuine effort to be better, to feel better, and it was working. The power of positive thinking was amazing.

"You look nice."

That voice. The deep baritone of it made the hairs on Jordyn's arms stand at attention. Jordyn spotted Zion leaning against her car, and she smiled at him. She'd asked Vadah a few times had she seen him after the gas station incident, and Vadah always told her no.

"Are you following me?"

A sexy smirk covered Zion's face. Clad in blue jeans with a white crew neck and denim Fila cap, he looked clean as ever. A simple yet stylish Jesus piece chain hung from his neck while Cartier wood grained glasses sat on his face. He was truly a Detroit nigga, and Jordyn had to admit that the Detroit boys had a style all their own.

"Fate keeps pushing us together, and I saw you walking in when I was leaving out. My aunt has a rental space in the building."

Jordyn nodded while smiling at him.

"And you waited forty-five minutes to see me?"

Zion cracked a smile.

"Hell yeah! We need to talk," he replied.

Jordyn pulled at the ends of her straight hair. She wore leggings with multi-colored Huaraches and an off the shoulder vintage Selena tee. She was looking to head home and get in a good smoke session before catching up on old episodes of *Sex & The City*.

"I don't know. So much time has passed and..."

Zion stepped off the car while staring at her.

"And I still think about you. I miss you, and I'm glad as fuck to see that you doing good." Zion stopped talking to grab Jordyn's hand. His hooded eyes bore into her as he spoke. "I'm sorry for disappearing like I did. Let me steal some of your time. *Please*," he pleaded.

Jordyn took a deep breath and exhaled.

"I guess. You can follow me to my place."

Zion smiled and let her hands go.

"Bet, I'm following you, beautiful," he happily replied.

Jordyn got into her car and nervously started it. She called Vadah as she pulled away from her therapist's building.

"Hey boo!" Vadah greeted, making her smile.

Jordyn cleared her throat. In her rearview mirror, she could see Zion in his truck following her.

"Zion was outside of my therapy appointment today waiting for me. He said he saw me going in, and he waited close to an hour for me to come out. Now he's following me to my place. What do I do?"

Vadah laughed.

"Ummmmmmm, you sit on the dick."

Jordyn laughed, not expecting Vadah to say that. Vadah joined in with her before turning serious.

"Okay, I'm sorry. I had a drink earlier with Quan. You need to tell him how hurt you were by him dipping off on you like that. That's what you need to do. I know he's fine as hell, but don't let that control the moment. Tell him how you feel," Vadah replied.

Jordyn nodded.

"Got it. Tell him how I feel," she repeated.

"Yes, and I think you'll be good. Call me when he leaves, and don't let him stay!"

Jordyn frowned as she drove home.

"I'm not letting him do that, so don't even worry," she replied before ending the call.

Thirty minutes later....

"Oh my God… wait!"

Zion shook his head as his tongue rapidly licked at Jordyn's clitoris. Jordyn's legs shook as her back bent off the coffee table. She'd stepped into her place with good intentions. She was ready to discuss the issue she had with Zion. However, one look at him, and all her good sense flew out of the window.

Zion was giving her a tongue lashing that her body couldn't ignore. The way he pleasured her was insane, and the way it made her body feel was unreal. Jordyn grabbed his head as her thighs shook uncontrollably.

Once she was done climaxing, Zion sat up and wiped his face as she attempted to catch her breath. Zion rubbed up and down her soft thighs before gently pulling her up.

"You okay?" he asked and chuckled.

Jordyn nodded. She stared at him lustfully as her pussy throbbed. She grabbed Zion's t-shirt and pulled him toward her. With his face inches from hers, she smiled lazily at him.

"Do you have a condom?"

Jordyn's question made Zion's dick go limp. He pushed her hand away and frowned at her. His hat, glasses, and jewelry had been tossed on her countertop in her kitchen along with his keys. As he stood to his feet, he glanced around for anything else that he might have taken off.

"Zion?"

Zion ignored Jordyn and slipped his shoes on. Jordyn stood up and pulled off her shirt. In her beautiful, naked glory, she walked over to Zion and grabbed his hand. The anger he felt shined through to his handsome face, making it contort into a scowl.

"I'm good. I need to go do some shit anyway," he said.

Jordyn stared up at him with a blank expression on her face.

"Are you mad 'cause I wanna have sex?"

Zion chuckled.

"Nah, I told you I just need to do some shit, but are you asking me to strap up because you fucking now?"

Jordyn let Zion's hand go and went over to her sofa. She sat down and glanced over at him. Her straight hair was sweated out at the edges. Her bright eyes were filled with lust, and her body was sweaty from her orgasm. She looked like everything Zion had been missing and dreaming about. Still, the thought of her being sexually active bothered him.

A lot.

"You fucking, Jordyn?" Zion asked again with his jaw tensing.

Jordyn nodded, and like the devil was fucking with her, Tye began to call her cell phone. Zion watched her as she grabbed the phone and answered it.

Jordyn swallowed hard as Zion stared her way.

"Hey, um, I'm going to just grab that weed from you another time," she said quietly.

Tye sighed. He intended to fuck his problems away with her, and now she was flaking out on him.

"Yeah, okay. You busy, baby?" Tye's loud, deep voice asked, booming through the speakers.

Zion's fist clenched before he took his shoes back off. He

walked over to Jordyn and grabbed her phone. Not giving it a second thought, he held it to his ear.

"Yeah, and you can lose her number, nigga," he said before ending the call.

Zion set Jordyn's phone down, and Jordyn shook her head. Tye was a cool nigga. He didn't do drama, so like she expected, he didn't call back. She watched Zion sit beside her, and she smiled at his ignorance.

"Can I tell you a story?"

Zion sat back and frowned. He was so fucking mad he didn't know what to do.

"I don't wanna hear no fucking story, ma," he grumbled, making her laugh.

Jordyn stood up and grabbed her roach box. She sparked up one of her tiny joints and joined Zion on the sofa. She turned her body toward him and took a few small hits before passing it over.

"It's about a girl who was and honestly still is lost. I mean, she's better now, but she has a long way to go. Anyway, I'm getting off topic. So, she met this man. He was so fine, Zion. Like sexy as fuck. So sexy it would make you go against your morals and fuck with him after you been fucking with his brother. That kind of fine. Things were cool. They chilled with each other and really vibed. Then shit went left.

"I'm not sure what happened, but he just stopped talking to her. She tried to call him for days, weeks, and even months. She went by his businesses, and they were closed. She was hurt. He was someone who she felt like she could rely on, and he gave her his ass to kiss. He walked away, and she was mad. She had around that time found out that her father up and moved and was no longer in Detroit either.

"That girl felt very alone, and she lashed out. She quit school, and she started partying hard. She fucked a few men. Got the hang of it and started loving it. It gave her a brief break from the madness that was her life. She started to hit rock bottom, and her family stepped in. Made her get her shit together, and well, that's how I got to this point."

"I'm not putting what I did on you, but don't make yourself the victim. I wanted to be something with you, Zion. I cried for months because of you, and I fucked a lot of niggas to get you out of my head. So yes, niggas gonna blow me up. Yes, I know how to take some dick, but you need to ask yourself what you did to prevent that from happening?"

Jordyn grabbed her small roach from Zion and stood up. She finished it off as she went into her bedroom.

Jordyn turned on some music, blackened out her bedroom, and turned on the star lights that hung over her bed. She lay in her bed as her small high washed over her. It wasn't her intention to be so blunt with Zion, but the more she thought of how he'd played her, the angrier she became.

"I was fucked up that day I pulled the gun on my brother. I was fucked up when I met you, Jordyn. I didn't like the shit I was thinking, ma. I didn't like the shit I'd done. I'd become someone I didn't know. I had to get better for my daughter. I fucked with you. I still do, but Zory will always come first. I had to get right for her before I ended up dead like her mom. I had to go to some intensive counseling treatments and just get my mind right. I had to let go of a lot of shit. Things I couldn't change and accept what happened. It wasn't about us. It was bigger than that because if I was still that same nigga, you would be too good for me anyway," Zion said, standing in the doorway.

Jordyn continued to stare up at the ceiling. She'd heard him loud and clear but was still hurt by the way he'd handled it.

"I understand. You had to look out for you and your daughter. It's good that you stepped up to make it right with her," she mumbled.

Zion walked into the room and took his clothes off. Once he was down to his boxers, he joined her on the bed and pulled her close to him. His touch seemed to sear into Jordyn's skin as he gripped her hips.

"But I missed you. I always thought about you, and I'm sorry. I'm sorry your pops dipped out, and I'm sorry I walked away from you. You're not alone."

Jordyn thought of her family and smiled.

"I know."

Zion leaned down, and gently, his lips brushed across hers.

"I won't walk away again," he promised before kissing her so hard it took her breath away.

Zion's kiss turned Jordyn's body on fire. She melted into her plush cover as he climbed on top of her managing to not pull his lips away from hers. Jordyn pulled him close to her and wrapped her legs around his body. Immediately, his large erection began to press against her.

"Ugh, Zion," she moaned when he pushed it into her.

She was still wet from climaxing earlier and the more he teased her, the wetter she became. Zion began to lick and suck on her neck before sliding his tongue down to her supple breast.

Jordyn closed her eyes and breathed hard as Zion sucked on her nipples. Between the weed and Zion, she was floating in the room. She'd never been so turned on in her life.

"Please put it in," she begged shamelessly.

Zion tugged at her nipple with his teeth before pulling it into his mouth and sucking on it. He pulled his dick out of his boxers and pressed it against her opening.

"J, you been fucking raw?" he inquired. Shit, fine or not, if she was getting down like that, then he would have to decline on the sex.

"No, I swear I haven't. Not even my first," she told him truthfully.

Zion looked up at her and into her eyes. Slowly he fed her his dick until he was fully seated inside her wet sex. Jordyn's eyes watered as she gazed up into his eyes. He was thick and long, but it wasn't the kind of dick that would rearrange your organs. No, Zion was the perfect size for her.

"You feel so good… mmm… fuck me," she begged before moving her hips.

Zion's head fell back as he enjoyed her tight walls. She was still fist tight, and the more she moved against him, the harder he got. Zion began to slowly push in and out of Jordyn until she tugged on his small beard. He looked down into her eyes to make sure she was good.

"I'm not as fragile as you think I am. I want you to fuck this pussy. Okay?"

Zion swallowed hard.

"You sure?"

Jordyn grinned up at him.

"Yeah, I'm sure. Tear this pussy up," she demanded sexily.

Zion pulled out of her and placed her on all fours. Jordyn tooted her round, soft, beautiful ass up in the air for him, and he thrust back into her hard. She whimpered as he pushed her back down as far as she would go. Zion slapped her ass, leaving a handprint before grabbing her hips. The thought of Jordyn giving up her pussy drove him insane. He knew he was to blame, but still, she was gone have to pay for doing that bullshit.

"From now on, you keep them fucking legs closed, you hear me?" he asked as he pounded into her.

With just a few hard thrusts, her walls were contracting around Zion. Her legs shook as she came, and Zion slapped her ass and watched it jiggle. She felt so good; there were no words to describe her.

"Did you hear what the fuck I said, J?" he asked and pulled her up.

Zion pulled her back close to his front and held her up by her neck. Jordyn whimpered as he drove his dick into her.

He was fucking her so good her eyes were leaking with tears.

"I heard you… my God, I heard you," she replied and came again.

Zion felt Jordyn get wetter, and he groaned. He massaged her neck before sticking two of his fingers into her mouth. Jordyn sucked on his fingers as he used his other hand to rub her clit.

Volts of pleasure shot through Jordyn as her body started to shudder.

"Zion… oh shit! Right there!" she yelled, and as she came again, he pushed her back down and long stroked her.

Zion slapped her ass as he watched her pant for air. She felt so good, better than he imagined. His hands dug into her soft skin as he plowed his dick into her.

"Can I cum in you?" he asked, feeling his balls tighten.

Jordyn nodded, thinking of her shot that she was on.

"Please do, shoot off inside of me," she purred, and he lost it.

Zion clenched his teeth together as he released everything he had deep inside her wet walls.

After fucking for two hours, Jordyn and Zion lay naked in the bed sharing a blunt. Zion didn't want any of her joints and ended up rolling his own blunt. Jordyn didn't wanna pass up on his strong ass weed, so like a team player, she shared it with him.

"She was the shit," Zion said as they listened to Nas and Lauryn Hill.

Jordyn frowned and glanced over at him.

"Was? She still is the shit. I love the rawness that you hear in her voice. You can feel it you know? *We'll walk right up to the sun we won't land,*" Jordyn sang soulfully.

Zion stopped hitting his blunt to stare at her. Jordyn's voice was amazing.

"Damn, I'm offended that you didn't sing for me before."

Jordyn blushed.

"I mean, maybe if you would have given me a few orgasms, I would have," she joked.

Zion chuckled. He was ready for another round, but he could tell Jordyn was sore, and he wasn't trying to literally beat her pussy out the frame.

"All you had to do was ask, but on some real shit, your voice is nice as fuck. Do Bezo know you can sing?"

Jordyn shook her head.

"No, and he won't. I don't wanna sing for people, Zion. I love my voice, and sometimes outsiders have a way of killing your dream. They'll turn it into something it's not. Use it against me and for money. I'm thankful that I have it, and I wanna keep it for me. They lucky I'm giving them my damn words to sing."

Zion passed her the blunt.

"You writing songs now too?"

Shyly, Jordyn nodded.

"Yes. My dad just signed me to his label, so I'm giving him a few hooks here and there," she revealed, telling him something that only a few people knew about. She hadn't even had the chance to tell Vadah the good news yet.

"That's what's up. I'm proud of you. You're doing really well for yourself, baby."

Jordyn hit the blunt, and his hand crept up her thigh. Gently, he massaged it as he glanced over at her.

"Have you looked for your pops since he moved?"

Jordyn blew the smoke out of her mouth and shook her head.

"I haven't, and I don't wanna talk about it. My best therapy for dealing with Rome is poetry. I'm getting it out, just in my own way, and my therapist said that's a good thing."

Zion leaned over and kissed her on the lips.

"It is," he replied, taking the blunt. He put it out and

pulled Jordyn onto his lap. His hands went to her ass as he stared at her face. "Who was that nigga that called?"

Jordyn playfully rolled her eyes. Now he asked. He'd been inside of her for hours and hadn't given a damn.

"A friend. I don't want or need a man."

Zion licked his lips.

"What if he needs you, though?"

Jordyn bit her bottom lip and sighed.

"I don't know what to tell him. He shouldn't need someone that's broken as fuck."

Zion grabbed her face and caressed her cheeks.

"Broken to you, but it's perfect to me," he said and kissed her tenderly.

Nineteen

"THAT SHIT SOUNDS GOOD. How would I do the chorus, though?"

Jordyn ignored Zion's third call before looking at the handsome singer.

Bezo was so amazing to her. He'd placed her in a studio in Detroit with some of the hottest up and coming singers and rappers on the Detroit music scene.

Jordyn was in her element. Music, she could do. It gave her such a joyous feeling. Jordyn knew that when it was right, magic could happen.

She listened to the song that was playing and started to hum the lyrics she'd just given Jody in her head. She still didn't like for people to know that she could sing.

"We got permission to sample that Isley song I was telling you about, so with that beat and my lyrics, I promise it will be magic. That shit is gonna bang, Jody, and have all them broads on your shit all summer long because this is definitely a summer song," she said, speaking like a professional.

A few of his boys nodded, and the song started over. The scene reminded Jordyn of her stepfather. As a family, they'd toured with him more times than she could count, and she'd also sat in on several studio sessions. Never in a million years did she think her life would follow down his path, but naturally, it had.

And she was cool with that.

"This shit is nice. You need to be writing for Beyoncé and shit," Jody said as he lit a blunt.

Jordyn grinned, wishing she would, then she thought of Erykah and SZA and *really* grinned. Jordyn loved all kinds of music, but she wasn't necessarily a commercial music writer. Her lyrics were raw, gritty, and deep on a level that many wouldn't openly relate to. Jordyn felt like Beyoncé might look past her songs, but someone like H.E.R just might touch them.

"I don't know. I'm not doing it for the money or fame. I just want the world to hear some real music. I'm lucky I have Bezo," she replied.

Jody nodded. He hit his blunt a few times before passing it to his little brother.

"Yeah, you are. That nigga is looking out, and he loves your ass. I remember you was on his one cover in that pink and purple mink and shit with your mom. That CD was a fucking classic too. I don't give a fuck if he's your real pops or not, music is in your blood, Jordyn. It was only right for you to do it," he told her and asked the producer to play the song back one more time.

Jordyn declined going to the club with Jody, trying to keep it professional, and ended up at home Face Timing her mom. Jordyn's mom, Logan, smiled at her as Jordyn spoke about her studio experience with Jody.

"It was so chill, Mom, and I knew what to do. Everything felt so right," Jordyn expressed with a smile.

"I'm so happy for you, baby. How is your therapy going?"

Jordyn sighed. She thought of Zion and shook her head.

"It's going well. I love the therapist you all hooked me up with. The only problem is Zion. He's back in my life, Mom, and I don't know how to feel about that. I wanna forgive him, then I don't," Jordyn replied.

"Did he explain why he walked away?" her mom asked.

Jordyn nodded while staring at her ceiling.

"Do you accept his apology?"

Jordyn shrugged. She did, but then she didn't. It was confusing even to her.

"He needed to work on himself for his daughter. Her mom was killed, and she'd been shot also, but she survived. Zion was angry behind it, and he said that he needed a break to get his mind right. I respect that. What I hate is how he did it. He cut me off with no reason as to why, and that still stings. I was falling in love with him," Jordyn said lowly.

Her mom cleared her throat.

"And you still love him, huh? I see how that could scare you. Even make you think of Rome, but don't put your issues with Rome onto Zion. If he's better and his apology is sincere, you should accept it. Especially if you still love him," her mom replied.

Jordyn closed her eyes as she pondered over her mother's words. She wanted to forgive Zion but something was stopping her from doing so.

Bezo: *That song you did for Jody was the shit. I knew you could do this J. I'm so proud of you.*

Jordyn smiled.

Thank you! She texted back. She scrolled down to her next message and shook her head.

Tye: *HMU. I miss you, beautiful, and I need that release. Only the kind you can give me sexy. Hit a nigga up and stop dodging me. My feelings lowkey hurt.*

Jordyn sighed as she re-read Tye's message. Zion grabbed her phone jokingly, and she quickly snatched it back. Zion stopped smiling and glared down at her.

"I was just fucking with you. What's going on? Didn't want me to see the nigga you were texting?"

Jordyn put her phone away and smoothed down her black midi skirt that extended to her knees. She then ran her hand over her sleek bun, and Zion shook his head.

"Why you acting so nervous? She's just a kid, ma," he said and glanced back down at her phone. "Who is he?" he probed.

Jordyn shook her head. She tried to walk ahead of Zion, and he slapped her on the ass before grabbing her arm. He pulled her back to him and placed his hand on the small of her back.

"I get it. I know I fucked up, but I'm sorry, and I won't do that shit ever again. I need you to look past what I did, so we can finish what we started, J," he told her.

Easier for you to say, Jordyn thought. She shook her head, not wanting to discuss it, and they walked up the steps leading to Zion's mother's home.

"Nigga, you late. We hungry as fuck," Zeke fussed and snatched the door open. Zeke looked down at Jordyn and shook his head before walking away.

Jordyn hesitated to walk into the tall, beautiful home, and Zion kissed the back of her head.

"Zeke is trying to get Dream back. He's not thinking about shit else plus he knows what's up with us. Relax," he told her and led her through the door.

Zion's mother's home smelled like heaven to Jordyn. Her stomach rumbled as she walked with Zion to the dining room. At a cherry oak table in the middle of the room was Zion's mother, his younger brother, Zeke, and Zory. Beside Zeke was a beautiful, brown skinned woman with slanted eyes and a pretty smile.

Jordyn saw the way the woman rested her hand on Zeke's leg, and she rolled her eyes. It was clear that Zeke was still on his bullshit because the woman looked nothing like the fiancée he was trying to get back.

"She's beautiful, Zion. Zory, do you know who this is?" Zion's mother Una asked.

Jordyn turned her attention to Una, and she smiled. Zion's mother was gorgeous. Zion had told her the story of how his mother was destined for a life of modeling when she'd been brutally attacked one night. The horrendous crime left her angry with her beauty, and she'd chosen to go to college instead and try to help shape children's' mind instead of putting her looks on display.

Una had dark, glossy skin with doe shaped, chestnut-colored eyes and tightly coiled curly hair that hung past her shoulders. She had the perfect bone structure, and Jordyn felt like Naomi Campbell would have had some serious competition had Una chosen to stay in the modeling industry.

"Hi everyone, and you are absolutely beautiful. Both of you are," Jordyn said and walked over to Zory.

She dropped down to her knees and looked at the small person who looked like the girl replica of her father.

Zory still wore her school uniform with two long pigtails and a shy smile on her light brown face. She gave Jordyn a small smile, and Jordyn noticed she wore purple polish.

"Is that your favorite color? I know that's one of mine," Jordyn playfully told her.

Zory grinned.

"It is. I love sparkle."

Jordyn's eyes widened, and she dramatically held her chest.

"Me too! I promise I told your daddy that."

Zory laughed with everyone else at the table minus Zeke.

"It is! Who are you to my daddy? My mommy is dead," Zory said, and Jordyn had to swallow hard.

"Yes, I know, and I'm his special friend."

Zory nodded, still staring at Jordyn. Zory reached out and gently touched the freckles on Jordyn's face.

"You're pretty," Zory told her.

Jordyn's heart did a different beat as she looked at the child before her.

"So are you. Can I eat with you all today?"

Zory laughed.

"Of course, silly," she replied, and everyone laughed while Una gave Zory a warning look, not caring for that word too much.

"No love for me, Zory?" Zion asked as he walked up to her.

Zory's little eyes lit up, and she jumped out of her seat. She ran into Zion's arms and hugged him tightly.

"Hi Daddy!" she squealed.

Jordyn stood up and watched them hug and talk to each other as if they were the only two in the room, and she smiled. She'd prayed for Zion and with him on that rock so many months ago, and like always, God heard them.

She was very happy to see him with his daughter.

"Please sit, sweetie," Una said, jarring her from her thoughts.

Jordyn, Zion, and Zory sat down, and Zeke's date looked at Jordyn.

"Do you model? I think I've seen you at some shows and online before," she said.

Jordyn nodded.

"I used to, but I don't anymore," she replied as Zion passed her a plate.

Zeke's date grinned at Jordyn.

"Well, you should keep modeling. Zeke is always asking me about it, but I love doing hair. I could never feel comfortable in front of a camera," she went on, and Jordyn simply nodded, not looking to do small talk with her.

Zeke's date picked up on her vibe and turned her attention back to Zeke.

"What do you do, Jordyn?" Una asked.

"I'm a songwriter, and I'm still deciding on if I will go back to school to get my degree."

Una nodded.

"Beauty and brains. I like that. School is important, and it's always nice to have a degree to fall back on, but that's amazing that you write songs. I love me some soulful music," Una said, and Zion and Zeke both shook their heads, hating the songs that their mother liked.

Una laughed and waved them off.

"Forget them. They don't know good music."

Zion pulled Jordyn close to him and kissed her on the cheek.

"Ma, she the coldest with the music. She was born to do it, and she's just like you. She hit them doobies and shit," he said, making Una's eyes widen.

Una tossed her napkin at him, and he chuckled.

"Don't tell my business, boy! What is wrong with you?" she asked him, and they all laughed.

Jordyn smiled as Zion and his mother began to go back and forth, and it made her think of her family. She missed them and knew that a flight home would be in her near future.

After dinner and a few family games, Zion, Zory, and Jordyn went back to his place. Zion put Zory in the tub and then the bed. As he read her a book, Jordyn stood in the doorway with her own pajamas on that she'd brought with her.

Zory rubbed her eyes as she looked up at Zion.

"Do you miss Mommy?" she asked him.

Zion nodded with sad eyes.

"I do, baby, every day, and she's here with us right now. You know that, don't you?"

Zory smiled as she rubbed his cheek.

"She is, Daddy, so don't be sad. Granny said that she would want us happy. Now I'm tired," she replied and yawned.

Zion kissed her goodnight and turned on her nightlight before leaving the room. Quietly, he walked with Jordyn to his bedroom. As they walked in, Jordyn's cell phone started to go off. Zion stripped out of his clothes and lit a blunt while Jordyn took Jody's call.

"I need one more song for the album. Everybody loves the other shit you did, and now I need more, baby," he told her.

Jordyn placed the call on speaker and grabbed her journal. She sifted through the pages in search of the one song she felt could fit him.

"I have one too. I'll text my dad so he can have the lawyer send you over the paperwork. Once that's out of the way, we can get in the studio again."

Jody cleared his throat.

"Yeah, have him do that, sexy. Why you ain't hit up the bar with us?" he asked, and Jordyn ignored the heated gaze that Zion pushed her way.

"I'll hit you up when the paperwork is done," she quickly said and ended the call.

Jordyn put her phone away along with her journal, and Zion cleared his throat.

"You fuck the niggas you write songs for?"

Jordyn leaned over and snatched his blunt out of his hand. She hated cigarillos but would deal with them when she had to.

"If I did, I wouldn't be here right now. We had a good day, Zion. Don't start looking for shit to fight about," she told him.

Zion chuckled. She sounded like a nigga to him.

"I guess I'ma lay down and let you fuck me to sleep too since you running shit around this bitch," he joked.

Jordyn hit his blunt a few times and shrugged as the smoke fell from between her pouty lips.

"Maybe I will," she mumbled.

Zion took the blunt and quietly seethed as he finished it off. Jordyn closed the bedroom door and killed the lights. She turned on her playlist titled *Love*. After she took off her clothes, she joined Zion on the bed. Jordyn climbed on top of him as his eyes connected with hers.

"Your daughter is amazing, and she's so strong. I love her already," she quietly said.

Zion nodded. He licked his lips as he eyed her.

"But do you still love me?" he asked in a low tone.

Jordyn ignored his question and pulled his limp penis out of his boxers. She gently rubbed it against her wetness, and in a matter of seconds, he was hard. Slowly, she slid onto him and closed her eyes. She couldn't say the words to him, she wasn't ready to, so she allowed the music to do it.

I'd go hungry, I'd go black and blue,
I'd go crawling down the avenue,
There's nothing that I wouldn't do
To make you feel my love.

Adele's gritty, soulful voice told him how she felt as Zion gripped her hips and drove his dick repeatedly into her until they both fell apart in each other's arms.

CHAPTER
Twenty

ONE SHOT.

Two shots.

Back to back, the drinks went down Jordyn's throat until she felt a burning in her small belly that told her to stop. The internet. She swore it was the fucking devil. At times it could be your friend, then in an instant, it would switch up and bring you some shit that you really didn't want.

Jordyn had woken up happy on a perfectly beautiful Saturday. Zion was out of town with his brother, and she was at home enjoying the warm May weather. She'd turned on her laptop, and on her granny's page, there he was. Rome had a surprise party in Detroit the night before for his birthday. The day he was born. A day she didn't even know about.

Tears; sad, angry, big, fucking tears fell down her freckled cheeks.

"I hate him. I fucking hate him," she said as she sat outside of her cousin's home.

With a bunch of investigations and shit like paying for addresses online, she'd found the family member's house that Rome was staying in. Jordyn leaned on the hood of her car with a bottle of white Remy. She was way past fucked up.

Zion's pistol was in one hand while the Remy bottle occupied the other one. Jordyn had never held a gun despite her mother's love of shooting them at the range. However, the moment she saw Rome's smiling face on her screen, she tore Zion's place up looking for it until she found it.

For an hour, she'd sat outside the home. For an hour, she'd mulled over every birthday that he hadn't bothered to show up for. Never had he spent her special day with her, but he wanted to celebrate his? Fuck no, she wasn't going to accept Rome shitting on her anymore.

"It was really nice, baby," Maniyla said as she walked outside with Rome.

Rome laughed until his eyes fell on his daughter. He tried to walk back in, and Jordyn stood up straight. With blurred vision, she aimed Zion's pistol at Rome and pulled the trigger.

Nothing.

That's what happened as she repeatedly did the act. Her sadness bubbled over, and once again, she was crying.

The safety had been put in place for a reason and had undoubtedly saved Rome's life. Maniyla stood to the side as Rome faced his fears and walked down the steps. He went over to his daughter. His beautiful daughter and grabbed the gun.

"Rome, you forgot your keys," his cousin Gerald said, stepping outside.

He spotted Jordyn then the weapon and frowned.

"Let them be," Maniyla said to him, and he nodded but didn't go back inside, wanting to make sure his cousin was okay.

"Wow, you're gorgeous," Rome said, looking down at Jordyn.

She had acquired her freckles and hair color from her mother's side of the family, but her skin color and eyes were all him. He was speechless at how beautiful she'd turned out to be.

Jordyn dropped the bottle of liquor. It fell to the ground and shattered, making the rest of it pour out. She wiped her eyes and looked up and down the street. Now that he was in front of her, she wasn't sure what to do. For so many days, she'd dreamed of this moment. She knew that he was there when she was younger, but she couldn't remember him. Couldn't recollect what his laugh sounded like or how it felt to have him around. He'd disappeared from her memory, and she was hurt.

Rome had hurt her and was still hurting her.

"Why?" she asked, finally bringing her red eyes to him.

Rome took a step back and cleared his throat. He looked good. Just as he did in the photos. He wore navy jeans with a short-sleeved Maison Margella shirt and Cole Hann loafers. His face still held a youthfulness to it despite him having an adult child.

"Your mom and her new nigga. They didn't want me around, and I tried. I tried to work with her. She was so fucking greedy. Always wanting some shit that I couldn't give. It was all about money with her, and then your fucking grandma jumped on my mom, and shit went bad. I had to let y'all go. I was tired of the drama and the stress," he said, stumbling over his words.

Excuses.

Jordyn shook her head. She looked down at her nude stiletto nails and bit her bottom lip. Rome cleared his throat as he looked her over again.

"I felt like it was best. That nigga your mom married has money. I saw the house he got, and I know you were raised well. I know that you graduated and shit like that, and I'm proud of you. You're doing good for yourself, and my mom she talks about you all the time. She told me you were writing songs now, and while I think that's not a stable career, I support it. I'm happy for you," he said.

Jordyn stood by, not giving him eye contact. She wished at that moment that she was a man. Only then could she be able to give him the type of ass whooping that he deserved.

She took a deep breath and exhaled.

"I spent twenty dollars today finding out where you were and a shit load of time on the internet. Twenty dollars was all it took when you could have found me for free. Everything I wanted to say to you is irrelevant. It doesn't matter anymore. You can give me the gun, and I won't shoot you," she told him.

Rome's chest ached. He shook his head, and Jordyn narrowed her eyes.

"I'm not going to shoot you, just give me the gun. It doesn't belong to me."

Rome shook his head again and placed the gun in the back of his pants. Jordyn was clearly drunk, and he refused to give her a loaded weapon.

"No, calm down. Listen, let's go in and talk," he calmly said to her.

Talk?

Those words angered her even more. Jordyn balled up her fist as she looked up at him.

"I don't wanna fucking talk to you! I didn't come here to *talk*, Rome. Why do you think I had that gun? I wanted to kill you! I wanted to take your sorry ass fucking life! That's what I wanted to do. You're a waste of space. You had a kid, stopped loving her, and moved on with your life. You're not shit! That fucking ant on the ground means more than you do. I will never sit down with you and talk like we're okay because we're not. We never will be, and it took me fucking my life up for me to see that. It took me moving here, fucking my pain away on random niggas for me to see that you're not shit, and you never will be. I will forget about you. I will pretend you don't exist the same way you've done me," Jordyn bitterly said. She walked up on Rome and looked him in the eyes. "I will have kids, and they won't know you. They won't ever hear your fucking name, and I'm fine with that. They will know of the real father that I have. The one who was man enough to love me when he didn't even make me. I pray that you die and burn in hell. That's my prayer for you, now give me that fucking gun," she demanded through gritted teeth.

Rome, with a heavy heart and watery eyes handed over Zion's gun. Jordyn walked to her car, gave him a parting smile before getting in, and she sped away. Instead of crying like she'd just done minutes before, she smiled. She wasn't happy. Who could be after realizing that the one person they always wished for wasn't real. She was heartbroken, but now that she knew, now that she had confirmation with her own two eyes that Rome wasn't the father for her, she was at peace. She felt like it was needed because now there were no more doubts, and the new ones that were on their way would quickly get shot down every time she thought about the day, she pulled up on him.

He wasn't who she wanted him to be, and the fact of the matter was, he never would be.

Jordyn lay on her granny's bed as she watched her apply her makeup. A week had passed since she'd seen Rome, and outside of her therapist, she hadn't told a soul. It was a moment she didn't care to dwell on. She went looking for answers, and she got them. She was still hurt, but it was easier now for her to accept that he wasn't there.

Her grandma Megan was going on a date, and she was excited to see who the man was. Megan looked amazing to have a grown daughter who had her own kids, and Jordyn was certain that the old and young men were still chasing her granny.

"Do you still think about Grandpa Deron?"

Megan smiled. The black shift dress she wore fit her snug just like she liked it. Her small glass of cognac rested on her vanity as she applied her mascara.

"All the time. I talked with him this morning. Let him know that this isn't personal, but it's needed. I'm lonely, baby, and I'm tired of denying my happiness for someone who isn't here in the physical. Even when he passed away, we weren't together, but it's that connection that made it hard for me to let go."

Jordyn smiled. She loved listening to people talk about love. Her eyes glanced down at her New Beginnings tattoo, and she briefly thought of Zion before shaking him out of her thoughts.

"Granny, do you regret anything with him?"

Megan laughed. She looked at Jordyn and nodded.

"Hell yes, I do. So many things, but I try not to dwell on that. It's really no point in doing so. What happened, happened, and there is nothing anyone can do to change it. You can move forward, baby. Who is he?"

Jordyn covered her face with her hands.

"Granny…" she whined, and Megan tossed a makeup brush at her.

"Don't Granny me. Talk, baby," she insisted.

Jordyn looked at her grandma and licked her lips. At that moment, she looked so much like her grandpa Deron that it made Megan's heart skip a beat. Deron had passed down his strong genes of the ginger hair and freckled skin to his kids, and of course, they kept the tradition going.

"His name is Zion, and he hurt me. Back when Rome was still here, Zion was a friend to me. We connected, Granny, and not in a sexual way. I wasn't even fucking him then… Oh, my god… Granny, I'm sorry!" Jordyn said and slapped her hand over her mouth.

Megan grabbed her black Gucci belt and rushed over to her grand baby. Playfully, she swatted her legs with the belt.

"You wasn't what? You better be a damn virgin until you say I Do, young lady," she said, and Jordyn laughed.

"Okay, okay! I'm sorry. We weren't even having intercourse. See, I'm a good girl," she mused, and Megan rolled her eyes, knowing better. "We were like really close. It's hard to explain, but he understood me then he cut me off. For over six months I didn't hear anything from him."

Megan sat on the bed.

"Was he locked up? If so, let his bum ass go. We don't do no jailbirds this way," she said, making Jordyn laugh.

"Granny, you act like granddaddy was a legit businessman."

Megan playfully popped Jordyn's leg again.

"He was. The Feds could be listening, girl," she jested.

Jordyn laughed harder.

"The Feds? Please stop, Granny, but seriously. Why should I give him a real chance? He could hurt me again."

Megan grabbed Jordyn's soft hand and gazed lovingly at her.

"When your grandfather stepped outside of our relationship to have a child, I was hurt. I couldn't move past that. I won't go into details, but know I raised all kinds of hell. I'm saying all of that to say that I was firm with my decision to not be with your grandfather. Can you look yourself in the mirror and be okay with not giving this boy another chance?"

Jordyn looked at her granny and frowned.

"He's far from a boy, Grandma."

Megan shook her head and stood up.

"Just like your momma. I was on that whiskey with her, and she must have been on that Arbor Mist with you," Megan replied.

Jordyn laughed and fell back on the bed. Something as simple as being up under her grandmother brought her so much joy.

After leaving her grandmother's place, Jordyn met up with Tye. Despite her worries, she was ready to give Zion another chance. Tye had been blowing her up, so she was going to spend some time with him and let him know that she was off the market. He was in downtown Detroit at one of his bars checking out a big party they were having for the night and wanted her to slide through for a drink. Jordyn answered the call from Zion as she approached the packed club.

Zion could hear the loud noise in her background, and he frowned.

"Where you at, ma? I wanted you to have dinner with Zory and me."

Jordyn frowned, hating he'd sprung the dinner news on her.

"I wish you would have told me earlier."

Zion chuckled.

"Shit, I hit you up three times, and you curved a nigga. It's not too late. We hitting up this little steakhouse in Birmingham. You wanna meet us up there?"

Jordyn sighed and glanced down at her clothes. She wore skin-tight ripped black jeans with a white top that read, *Your Loss* and wedge heels. Her hair was slicked down in the front and in a huge afro ponytail that looked sexy on her. She wore oversized hoop earrings with matte soft pink lipstick.

"Maybe next time," she said, knowing that she needed to cut Tye off so he could stop blowing her phone up.

Tye had gone from being her chill nigga to a pest overnight.

Vadah had told her that all niggas did that when they felt like a new nigga was around.

"Damn… straight like that, huh? You gone curve me and my daughter, J?" he asked with anger in his tone.

Tye spotted Jordyn's voluptuous ass and walked up behind her. He hugged her from the back and wrapped his arms around her waist.

"There go my, J," he said loud enough for Zion to hear him.

Jordyn sighed, knowing Zion was gone' be pissed.

"I see what type of shit you on. I'll fuck with you another time, and don't forget what you promised me either," he said before hanging up in her face.

Jordyn put her phone away and frowned.

"I see that nigga mad. Fuck him. He had his time, now you belong to me. Come on, sexy," he said and ushered her into the club.

Like always, Tye showered Jordyn with attention. Zion called Jordyn back twice, and she declined his calls. She took a few shots with Tye to ease her nerves before he placed some presents on her lap. Jordyn stared down at the dark orange packaging, wondering why he'd felt the need to grab her something out of the Louie store.

"Is it my birthday?" she asked and smiled.

Tye laughed. He looked handsome like always, dressed in black jeans with a red and white Pierre Balmain tee and black Givenchy sneakers. His burst fade was lined up per usual, as was his goatee. He wore this serious look on his handsome face that he didn't usually have with Jordyn.

"I was just thinking about you. I felt like a nigga was coming for something I wanted for me, so I knew I had to step my shit up. Look in the bag," he told her.

For him? Since when have your ass wanted anything more than pussy?

Jordyn shook her head to clear her thoughts and pulled two dust bags out of the shopping bag. In one was a large purse, and in the other was the matching wallet. Jordyn didn't have to look at the price tag to know he'd dropped some money on them. She smiled, absolutely loving how beautiful the gifts were, and Tye sat closer to her. His warm breath fanned against her skin before he kissed her cheek.

"I'm sorry 'bout the shit I said about your mom. I was blowed, and I won't joke like that again. You on some exclusive shit now with this nigga, ma? I can't even get you to go on a fucking date with me, and now you letting this nigga track your moves? What's good, Jordyn?"

The hostility in Tye's tone made Jordyn frown. She cleared her throat as she placed the items, he'd gotten her back in the bag. She needed to let him know what was up so she could go to see Zion.

"Aye, Tye! That nigga Bezo just walked in the building, dog!" a security guard excitedly said, and Tye jumped up.

Jordyn started to rock her leg, knowing her stepdad was gone' shit a brick when he saw her.

"I should just leave. I should have went to that damn steakhouse. I need to take that bag and dip off before he—"

"Welcome to my club, nigga!" Tye said, pulling Jordyn out of her thoughts.

Jordyn started to sweat as she watched Tye step to the side and let Bezo and his security, who she knew as family, step in. Bezo was on chill mode until he spotted Jordyn. His jaw tensed as he glared down at her.

"What the fuck you doing here? Why you chilling with this old ass nigga!"

"Nigga, this me." Tye chuckled.

Tye went over to Jordyn and sat down. He pulled her close to his side and smiled. Bezo moved swiftly in knocking the smile off his fucking face with a clean punch, and he didn't let up. VIP immediately turned into chaos, and Jordyn was pulled out of the section by one of Bezo's people. He carried her out of the club as the music stopped, and the lights cut on.

"Go straight home. We'll be by in a minute, Jordyn," Bear said before rushing back into the club.

Confused and still in a state of shock, Jordyn rushed to her car and got in. She tried to call her mom while she drove home but couldn't get through, so she called her grandma Megan.

Megan took the call on the first ring.

"Hey, baby. I'm about to have some coffee with my date. I'll call you when he leaves. He was just gone' help me organize the boxes in my shoe closet," Megan went on to explain, making Jordyn shake her head.

I can't believe this lady is still having sex. Ugh!

Jordyn held in her laugh, not wanting to put her grandma on blast.

"Okay, Granny," she replied and hung up.

Jordyn was soon pulling up to her place and exiting her car. As she headed for her front door, Zion emerged from his Lincoln truck. A scowl sat on his handsome face as he walked up behind her.

"You didn't see me fucking calling you, Jordyn?" he angrily asked.

Jordyn spun around at the sound of his voice and accidentally dropped her keys. Her heart pounded in her chest as she glared up at him.

"I thought you was with your daughter?"

Zion nodded. He looked her outfit over and swallowed hard. To know she'd been out with some nigga looking the way she did hit him hard. He wanted to be the only man lucky enough to have her time.

"She's asleep in the car. I can't fucking believe you, man."

Jordyn's head snapped back, and she laughed.

"Believe me? What the fuck did you expect me to do, Zion? Huh? You left me! I called you for months!" she yelled with her emotions bubbling over. Zion dropped his head, and she rushed up to him. Jordyn pushed him as hard as she could, but it was like hitting a wall. His stance never changed. "You knew what I was dealing with! I didn't hide my shit like you did. I told you...." Jordyn's sad tears slipped from her eyes. She pushed him again, and he finally brought his eyes to hers. "You're just like him, Zion. You gave me all this hope, and, in the end, you left me. It broke my fucking heart," she said, and he pulled her into his arms.

Zion hugged her tightly. He wanted her to feel his love. Know that he was too fucked up to love her the way she wanted to be loved. The sad fact was that he didn't love himself at the time, so he was incapable of loving her. He didn't have it in him to give. He was empty, depleted of the beautiful emotion, and the more he stayed around her, the clearer it became to him. That the only way he could have her and his daughter was for him to be a better man.

"I'm sorry, Jordyn. I'm really fucking sorry, baby. I needed to get better, and it had nothing to do with not wanting to be with you. I never intended to hurt you in any kind of way. I love you," he whispered to her.

Jordyn wept into his shirt, and Zion hugged her even tighter.

"You had become everything I had ever wanted in a woman, J. The time was just all fucked up. I was really in a bad place, baby. I couldn't keep moving like that because eventually, that shit would have killed me. I wanted to be better for both of y'all," he confessed.

Jordyn nodded.

She understood.

"I get it. I'm just scared. Because of Rome, it makes me question men. Wonder if their intentions are good, you know? It makes me feel like something is wrong with me because I wasn't even good enough for my own daddy to love me."

Zion grabbed Jordyn's face and made her peer up at him.

"You are. I love you, and I don't even deserve you, but I do. Even when you were constantly telling me how fucked up you were, you were changing for the better. You gotta give us a real chance, J. I will never walk away from you again, ma. I swear," he promised her.

Jordyn looked up at him again as two cars sped into the parking lot.

"What the fuck is going on, baby?" Zion asked, pushing her behind him.

Jordyn remembered Tye and Bezo, and her stomach dropped.

"Um… um…"

"Lil nigga, did you follow me here?" Bezo asked, jumping out of his car and walking toward Tye's black Range Rover.

Tye emerged from his truck with a swollen eye. He looked at Bezo and shook his head.

"I told you I would fall back if she wants me to. I'm trying to be respectful, but you pushing it. I got shooters on standby, nigga, and they always going for the head," he warned Bezo.

Bezo smiled at him and nodded. He wasn't worried about shit Tye was saying to him. He knew about Tye and his street status, hence the reason he didn't want him laying up with his daughter.

"I ain't one of these lil niggas out here. You better ask about me, muthafucka. Real killers don't do no talking," he replied.

As Jordyn watched everything go down, Zion stood stuck in his spot. He felt as if time was standing still for him.

Jordyn, his Jordyn was fucking with Tye? Tyshawn? Nah, couldn't be.

"You remember me, nigga?" Zion asked, stepping away from Jordyn.

Tye stopped glaring at Bezo to look over at Zion. His mind moved quickly to see who the nigga was. Shit, he had a few enemies, but he couldn't place a name to the face that was before him. Because Zion looked like he was ready to get down, it made Tye pull his strap out.

Seeing the gun made Bezo's bodyguard hop out the truck with his own weapon out. He went over to Jordyn as the smallest, prettiest little girl one could ever see emerged from Zion's Infiniti truck.

Zory rubbed her eyes as she unknowingly stepped into the middle of the mayhem.

"Daddy," she said quietly, and Tye glanced down at her.

Her face, he knew her. Had seen her a few times with one of his old hustlers, Jeremy. The same nigga who stole a bunch of coke from him and some money. He remembered placing a price on his head. Tye remembered his cousin saying how shit went wrong, and he had to cancel Jeremy and his bitch. How he also had to clip the kid. Tye was mad about him shooting a child, but the shit had been done, so he let it slide.

Tye aimed his gun at Zion, knowing that he would have to end his life as well.

"You was gunning for me a while back, right? Tying up my people, even killed my lil homie, Shane," Tye said, making Jordyn look at Zion with wide eyes.

Bezo's security grabbed Jordyn as she continued to stare at Zion. The quiet that had fallen over the parking lot was maddening. She could feel that shit was only going to get worse.

"Zion, please," she begged, and Tye looked at her.

Did he love her? No, but he cared, and his ego couldn't accept someone like Zion having Jordyn. No, Tye knew she belonged with a boss like him. Not a bum ass nigga who had dispensaries.

"Jordyn. Can I talk to you for a minute?" Tye asked and licked his lips.

"Aye, Bear, take Jordyn and the girl into her place," Bezo said, pulling his own gun out.

He was only a rapper, but he would never get caught without his gun. Niggas were too crazy, and he had too much to lose.

"Aigh't," Bear grunted before picking up Jordyn and snatching up Zion's daughter, Zory.

Jordyn didn't bother to get down because Bear was the biggest man she'd ever known. Hell, he would tower over Shaq if they stood face to face. Instead, she peered over his shoulder at Zion as Bezo spoke calmly to both men.

Bear took them into the building and had to rush back outside to grab Jordyn's keys. Jordyn looked down at the precious little six-year-old who was starting to cry, and she picked her up.

Zory's small body shook as Jordyn held her in her arms.

"I'm scared," she whispered.

Jordyn rubbed her back.

"It's okay. Everything will be okay," Jordyn told her, and the sound of gunfire made both of them scream.

"Oh my god... oh my god," Jordyn said and dropped to her knees.

She protectively covered Zory as her small apartment complex turned into the Wild, Wild, West.

Suddenly, the gunfire stopped, and her neighbors in the apartment building started to open their doors. Jordyn slowly stood up, and the building door was snatched open.

Zion stood on the other end of the door with a forlorn look on his handsome face. Zory ran to him, and he picked her up as he looked Jordyn's way.

"J," he said quietly.

The way he acted was alarming to Jordyn. Jordyn pushed past him and walked outside. Tye was gone along with his truck. Bear carried Bezo to his vehicle as he struggled to breathe.

Jordyn's heart dropped at the sight of the only father she'd ever known being hurt.

"Dad," she whispered as she cried.

"Come on, J!" Bear shouted.

Jordyn ran to the truck and got in. Bear quickly put Bezo in and sped away.

The ride to the hospital was a quiet one. Jordyn glanced back at Bezo as he lay across the backseat with his eyes closed.

"I'm so sorry. I'm so sorry," she said quietly over and over again.

Bezo shook his head. His body was on fire. He'd never been shot before, and it wasn't no shit he wanted to experience again.

"Relax, baby girl," he said in a raspy voice.

"Don't talk, nigga, just be cool," Bear said, getting choked up himself.

Jordyn continued to stare at Bezo until Bear pulled up at the hospital. They went in through the emergency door, and Bezo was immediately taken to the back. Bear called up Jordyn's mother while Jordyn sat quietly beside him. She felt like everything was her fault.

Jordyn thought back to the first time she'd learned how to rollerblade and how scary it was. Bezo had been the perfect father to her, even when she hadn't been the best child. Her tears fell freely down her flushed face, and Bear pulled her to his side. He was not only Bezo's bodyguard but his first cousin.

"He's cool. They went in and out. You know he not gone' let this shit take him away from y'all," he assured her.

Jordyn nodded, still feeling like shit. She rested her head

on Bear, and soon the room was filled with her grandmother Megan along with her aunt Jerricka, who was her mom's best friend.

As Zion walked through the door, Jordyn stood up. Zion was kid less and wearing a look of sadness on his face as well. He moved past Jordyn and went over to Bear. Quietly, he exchanged words with him, and Bear patted his arm. Zion then went to Jordyn and pulled her into a tight embrace.

"I'm sorry. It's all my fault," he told her.

Zion took Jordyn over to some seats a few rows away from everyone, and he sighed.

"He was protecting me, J. I don't know how, but he just knew Tye bitch ass was about to shoot me, so he ran to me and pushed me out the way. Tye hit him twice, and he fell on me. Then Bear started blasting at Tye, and shit got crazy. Tye still was able to leave. I don't know if he was hit, though. I feel so fucked up behind this shit, man. It's all my fault," Zion said and dropped his head.

Jordyn sat next to him speechless. Bezo had risked his life for Zion. She shook her head and rubbed Zion's back.

For three hours, Jordyn and her loved ones waited to hear from someone at the hospital on the status of Bezo. It wasn't until Jordyn was falling asleep that a doctor came out to speak to them. Jordyn stood beside Bear as they were notified of his injuries.

"He needs rest, and we will keep him. We were able to remove both bullets. However, he lost a lot of blood. When his wife arrives, she'll be able to see him."

Jordyn sighed with relief.

"But he's okay, right?" she asked worriedly.

The doctor nodded.

"Yes, he's stable," the doctor replied before walking away.

Jordyn hugged Bear then her grandmother. As she went to embrace Zion, her mother and siblings along with her auntie

Kolbee rushed into the room. Jordyn looked at her mom's worried face, and her worries entered her once again.

"Mom, I swear I didn't want any of this to happen! I'm so sorry!" she yelled as she ran toward her.

Logan shook her head while hugging her tightly.

"Where is he?" she hurriedly asked.

"Let me show you," Bear said and pulled Logan away.

Jordyn embraced the rest of her family before following her mom. When Jordyn entered the hospital room, her mom was standing beside the hospital bed holding Bezo's hand. He looked at her and gave her a weak smile, which made Jordyn break down.

Jordyn ran to his side and hugged him gently.

"I'm so sorry! I never meant for any of this to happen to you, Daddy," she said as he rubbed her back.

Bezo coughed, and she pulled back and looked at him.

"I'm fine, J. You gotta calm down before you end up in here for high blood pressure and shit. I saw that look in Tye's eyes, and I knew. I knew he was gone' hit your friend. I had to at least try to save him, but damn, I didn't expect to get shot. I'm good, though, and I don't want you to blame yourself. I just need you to promise me one thing," he said and looked up at her.

Jordyn wiped her face.

"What's that?"

"I need you to love yourself more, baby girl. We all see the changes, and we're proud of you, but you gotta do better. Tye got businesses, but he's a street nigga. I could tell you a million fucking stories I done heard about him. You could get caught up in his shit, then you'd be the one on the receiving end of a gun.

"Stop looking for these niggas to give you the love that you already have. You feeling lonely, come home. You wanna go out and don't have nobody to go with you, call Jerricka up. You know her crazy ass can't keep no man. Stop feeling the need to be up under some nigga. Don't sell yourself short like that, J. Shit, the way that nigga was eyeing you at your place, I can see he been hit by the Flint woman bug anyway," he said, and Jordyn nodded before smiling.

"What Flint woman bug?" Logan asked Bezo.

Bezo looked at her and licked his lips. The love and adoration he had for her showed in his eyes.

"You know what I'm talking about. That shit that makes you feel like you gone' lose your mind if you don't have that woman in your life. That's how he was looking at our daughter," he replied.

Jordyn shook her head as her cheeks flushed. She looked at her mom and saw that her mom was peering at her intently.

"Are you mad at me, Mom?" she asked.

Her mom nodded while holding her husband's hand.

"I'm fucking furious with you. Bellamy could have been killed tonight, Jordyn. I know he isn't Rome, but he's your father. The only fucking man who has ever gave a damn about you. This shit stops today, Jordyn. Do you hear me?" her mom asked with gritted teeth.

Jordyn swallowed hard. She nodded as her eyes watered, and her mom sighed.

"You stay far away from that guy who shot your dad and change your cell phone number first thing in the morning. Until you're out of that apartment, you will also be with my mom or back home in Atlanta. We're not taking any chances until he's apprehended."

Bezo chuckled at Logan's choice of words.

"Apprehended? Baby, I'ma handle that—"

Logan covered his mouth and shut him up, which made him laugh harder. Jordyn watched the two go back and forth, flirting with each other, and it made her smile. Bezo was the perfect man for her mom, and she knew in her heart that Zion was the perfect man for her.

Epilogue

"MY WHOLE LIFE, I been waiting for this. Making music was always in me. I just had to embrace it. This was my last album, and I'm nothing like the legendary Hov. When I say I'm done, I mean that shit. But this isn't just about me. It's about my family. My fans and the people who were riding with me when I was selling my CDs out the back of my stolen car. I been at the bottom more times than I could count, but I made it. I kept at it, and here I am. I wanna be inspiration for people like me. Young boys living in the hood who feel like the streets are their only way out. I'm living proof that you can make it, and you don't have to sell drugs to make it happen."

Bezo stopped talking, and his eyes connected with Logan's. He smiled at her before he looked at his children who all sat in the front row with her. His son was in his first year of college on his basketball scholarship. Bellamy Jr. was destined for greatness. Then, there was little miss Toni who was already embracing her dancing talent. Finally, he looked at Jordyn, and he cleared his throat.

"I wanna also thank my daughter. First, before I call her up, let me say she's taken by that dude sitting next to her.

Peep that ring that's on her finger, and she ain't have to get pregnant for him to drop on that knee either," Bezo said, and everyone in the grand room clapped.

Bezo was positive his time was close to being up, but he didn't give a damn. They were celebrating him with an award for album of the year, so they were going to celebrate his baby too whether they wanted to or not.

"Come here, baby girl," he said, and the spotlight went to a radiant Jordyn.

Jordyn blushed, feeling all eyes on her, and Zion lovingly kissed her cheek. He was clad in a black Tom Ford wetsuit while she wore a mustard colored Versace mermaid gown with her long red hair in soft curls that spiraled down her back.

She hugged Zion and slowly stood up.

Everyone began to clap while women admired her beauty, and men, well they admired everything about her.

Bezo met her halfway and helped her walk up the steps. On Jordyn's finger was her princess cut diamond that Zion had given to her two months ago while visiting Hawaii again, and the smile that sat on her face could be seen a mile away.

It was clear that she was a woman who was madly in love.

"Everyone, this is my daughter, Jordyn. She wrote the chorus for all my songs on my album, and she sang the poem at the beginning of it. She's the future of soul R&B, and I pray I'm alive to see her get inducted into the Hall of Fame because I know it's coming. Jordyn tell them who you are," Bezo said, staring down at her.

Jordyn looked up at him and swallowed hard. Her pretty, enchanting eyes that were decorated with sparkly eyeshadow watered. She whispered a tender *thank you, Daddy*, and walked up to the mic.

"Hi..." Jordyn laughed nervously. "I'm extremely nervous. I never thought in a million years that my dad would call me up on stage. I first have to thank him for believing in me. I wasn't always the easiest child to deal with, but his love for me and his other children never wavered. I'm grateful to have him in my life," she said, and her eyes connected with her mother.

Logan smiled at her while wiping away a stray tear.

"I wrote all of those lyrics from the heart. Some of those songs come from pain, and some from happiness. I now know that my passion for music came from my dad. Watching him rap and being in this element did it for me. I loved it as a kid, and I love it now, but this isn't about me. This is about the man who has released over four independent projects and sold millions of records. He's topped chart after chart while being an amazing husband and father. This is about *my* daddy who I love with all my heart. Nobody deserves this album of the year award more than he does," she said, and Bezo pulled her into his arms while the crowd rose to their feet and clapped for him.

A beautiful Vadah and Quan, who were seated behind Zion, stood with the crowd and clapped for Bezo and Jordyn as well. The two had been in attendance to see the legendary moment, and Vadah was so proud of her girl.

Jordyn cried happy tears into his suit as she embraced Bezo. Since seeing Rome and pulling a gun on him, she hadn't tried to see him again. And she wouldn't. For Jordyn, life was good. She had Zion and Zory. She had her music, her family, and her God. She had peace. Peace that only comes when you know why you were placed on earth and when you start to live your passion. She was happy, and she wasn't going to complain because she remembered what it was like to be sad, depressed, and heartbroken.

That shit felt like hell, and never again did she wanna live that way. She was also happy for her friend. Vadah's business was now open and doing extremely well. She had been on the news because of it and was looking to open another building in the near future. Vadah and Quan were now happily together and living a peaceful, private, quiet life, just how they both liked it.

Both Jordyn and Vadah were free. Free from pain, free from stress, and free from worry. They were both living with healed hearts, and to them, nothing could top that.

www.ingramcontent.com/pod-product-compliance
Lightning Source LLC
Chambersburg PA
CBHW052000150726
47999CB00004B/1455